"COMPLETE MAGIC"

"A daring accomplishment . . . Nathan keeps alive the tradition of enchantment . . . This novel, as all enduring novels, may be read on any level from entertainment to prophecy. It will, I am certain, bring many new readers to this great storyteller, to find in his novels a world celebrating tenderness, love, mystery"

STONECLIFF
ROBERT NATHAN

POPULAR LIBRARY • NEW YORK

To *Minnie*

Author's Note

There is, actually, a Los Olivos
—but not where I have placed
it. And if there is, somewhere,
an Edward Granville—and if
he has a wife—he is unknown
to me by that name.

But to the lover, beauty is his love,
His heart's dear mistress, ever at his side;
She is the blue bright wind of heaven above,
The light of evening on the valleys wide.
She is the sea, she is the swifter tide
Of narrower waters, and the forest green;
In all his courses, beauty is his guide,
She goes before him, she is heard and seen,
And has a body. Let the lover tell
Whose voice he hears in music's sweetest part;
He knows the face of beauty, knows it well,
She is his friend, the treasurer of his heart,
Which on the earth like benediction pours
A light he loves, a spirit he adores.

"For insofar as Matter is controlled by Spirit, so can Spirit draw forth from itself certain living forms, which, being immaterial, do then become familiar, passing among us like creatures; by which Magic we are caused to remember the serpent sleeping by the pool, and among the flowering bushes, a dreaming of nymphs."

BERNARD DE TREVES

CHAPTER

1

I have been sitting here at my desk with the last page of my book in front of me—my book, still untitled, the biography of the novelist Edward Granville. It is all done, complete, with names and dates and places, facts gathered from many sources, including Stonecliff itself. And yet in a real sense it is not done at all, for I know that the life of the book itself has escaped me; the mystery that baffled me then eludes me still.

I must try to remember when it all began.

I was driving slowly along the coast toward Los Olivos, climbing and winding along the great cliffs which rose stony and broken from the sea. Far below me the tide washed in on the shingle in long, slow curves of greenish foam. It was mid-afternoon, the air was fresh, there was a sea-smell in it, and another smell of cypress and rocks and sweet-grass in the sun. Perhaps it was the nature of my errand which made me think of this part of the coast as Granville country; at one point, looking up, I thought I caught a glimpse of a young woman silhouetted for a moment against the wind-clear blue of the sky; but when I looked again, she was gone.

I was to stay at Stonecliff for a few days, to take notes, ask questions, and in general familiarize myself with the life of the novelist who had been called the last of the Academicians. My visit had been arranged by his publishers, Messers Hunter and Sons, and I looked forward to meeting a man who had been the friend of so many of the great writers of the past. His own life was well known—up to a point; but he had retreated years ago to these same lonely cliffs, from which, every two years, he sent a novel to his publishers. He was known to have married in middle-age, but few people had seen his wife, or remembered her very clearly; her name was Virginia, and as far as anyone knew, they were still together, living in a solitude which—apparently—satisfied them both. He had few visitors; most people supposed him already dead, and it was to remedy this mistake and to bring him before the public again that his publishers had arranged for me to write the definitive biography.

I had been given careful instructions, and had no difficulty in finding the house which sat high on a ledge overlooking a great expanse of ocean. It was large, and built of rough stone, with a flagged terrace facing the sea; two large cypress trees stood at either corner of the terrace, along whose low stone balustrade a straggle of climbing roses anchored themselves against the wind.

I was greeted at the front door by Granville himself, who led me into the study which looked out, not upon the sea as I would have expected, but on a quiet garden in the rear, open to the morning sun, but now in shadow, and set about with flowering vines, camellias, azaleas, rhododendrons, and birds of paradise in wooden tubs. It was here—as I later learned—that he did his writing, finding it easier to marshal his thoughts when gazing out at a small frame of comfort than when faced by a limitless expanse of sea and sky.

"You are Mr. Robb," he said, studying me.

He stood with his back to the window, so that I was in full light; but he soon appeared to be satisfied with what he saw, for he nodded his head, and declared,

"I have been expecting you. I will show you to your room now."

He was, I realized, taller than I had imagined. From his biography in *Who's Who*, I knew him to be in his late sixties, but he appeared younger. There was something withdrawn and somber about him, but his eyes were gentle and not without humor. I had also expected him to have a beard, but he was clean-shaven, though his skin was lined and darkened by sun and wind.

"What shall I call you?" he asked, as we went up the stairs to the room I was to have during my visit.

I replied that my name was Michael. "Then to-day," he said, "you will be Mr. Robb. And tomorrow, after breakfast, you will be Michael."

He turned and gave me a quick smile. "I do not believe in too sudden familiarity," he said. I could not decide whether he was serious or not, but I knew that I would never call him anything but Mr. Granville.

My room, at the opposite end of the house from his own, was large and comfortable, the walls unadorned except for one good Zajac from the painter's Mexican period, opposite the window which looked out at the cliffs to the north. A Zuni Indian rug warmed the floor, which was of oak, as was the big, old-fashioned bed and the writing table already set out with paper, pencils, and note books.

I unpacked, and put away my things; and all the while I felt that curious sensation of waiting and listening which I always feel in a strange house. I went to the window and leaned out, gazing up at the rocky slopes to the north, already shadowy, their color lost in the approaching twilight. The air was cold, and I smelled the sweet, bruised fragrance of jasmine, and the spiky smell of the little desert flowers among the rocks. I could hear the long, low grumble of the sea far below at the foot of the cliffs. I felt the loneliness of the evening, the darkening air and the small wind, the emptiness of the land . . . and I thought of all the brave, sad, lonely, merry people of Granville's stories, the loving girls, whose ghosts must roam those cliffs and haunt the gardens of oak and cypress in which they had lived their insubstantial lives . . .

A cold wind blew down the slopes from the north, and I was glad to turn back to the room again, and switch on the lights.

When I came downstairs, a fire was already burning cheerfully in the living room; and after a martini for me, and a sherry for Mr. Granville, he led me into a small, formal dining-room, where a refectory table in the Spanish style, with heavy, carved legs, had been laid for two. The room was lit by candle-light which was reflected in the hurricane lanterns at either end of the buffet, in the Victorian silver tea service, and in the dark panelling of the walls. The food, served by an old Mexican woman, was plain and good: a bean soup, a roast of beef, vegetables, a salad, and coffee in small, delicate, Sèvres cups. With dinner we were served a light, dry wine.

My host apologized for the fact that his wife was not present. "Virginia—Mrs. Granville—" he explained, "is away for a while. I hope that you will not be too uncomfortable in her absence."

I found him pleasant, and easy to get along with. He talked freely about his work, and about himself—though he told me, actually, nothing that I didn't already know, for his life, to a certain point, was to be found in the encyclopedias. But when I asked him why he had given up his home in the city to come to live in this lonely part of the country, his face took on an expression at once obstinate and secret. "I do not find it lonely, Mr. Robb," he said. "I create my own society."

It seemed to me, then, the usual answer of a novelist, and I took it in the literary sense. "I suppose every writer creates his own society, more or less," I said.

He gave me a long, quiet look across the table. I thought that he wanted to tell me something, but whatever it was, he apparently changed his mind, for he merely remarked,

"Yes."

After a moment or two he roused himself as though with an effort. "Tell me, Mr. Robb," he said; "do you believe that God is dead?"

I was unable to conceal my surprise. "To tell you the truth," I said, "I have never thought about it. Though considering the way things are in the world today . . ."

"Were they better in the past?"

The question stopped me; after all, how could I answer it? People probably lived in anguish— and died in fear—in the Middle Ages, too.

He noticed my confusion, and held up a reassuring hand. "I ought not to have asked you that question," he said; "and besides, it is of no importance. The theory that God is dead is popular today in certain theological circles. Yet everywhere one sees before him, day after day, the act of creation."

He toyed for a moment with his glass, studying the reflection of candle-light in the crystal. "Perhaps it goes on by itself," I said idly; "having once been set in motion. Nature . . ."

"I was speaking about imagination," he said. "Not chemistry."

On this, to me, rather obvious note, I thought it the right moment to ask him a few questions about his own method of creation. "Tell me," I asked; "are they real, the people in your books?"

He was obviously taken aback by my question, for he looked up sharply. "What I mean is," I floundered a little, "have you known these people in your actual life? Or do they exist simply in your own mind . . . ?"

He shook his head, as though the subject puzzled him. "I have known them," he said impatiently. "I have lived with them."

"Then," I said, "they are not imaginary?"

"No," he said, "they are not imaginary."

After we had finished our coffee, and he had lighted his cigar, he beckoned me out to the terrace. The air was cold and moist, the heavens clear and starry overhead; the sea moved in deeper darkness below us; and again as from the window of my room, I smelled the over-sweet fragrance of jasmine.

We walked quietly up and down for a few moments, when Granville suddenly stopped, and pointing to a dark, starless space in the sky above us, declared,

"In that direction, a billion light-years away, lies a galaxy without a name. It is one of how many we do not know, and larger than our own which includes all the stars that can be seen in the sky."

He pulled for a moment on his cigar, and the fiery rim behind the ash glowed and dimmed. "In the enormous space of the cosmos," he remarked, "that galaxy is no more than the spark of my cigar."

He continued thoughtfully,

"Even to describe the universe is impossible. And to comprehend it is beyond the reaches of the mind. But to have created it! What incredible imagination!

"The question is: what materials did He have to begin with?"

He leaned for a moment on the balustrade, staring out at the night. "I, too," he said at last, "use whatever is at hand. I make a young woman out of fog and rain and flowering bushes . . . and love and memory."

He smiled, a little shyly. "At first I am the only one to see her," he said. "But then one day she is seen by other people too; and young lovers look at each other, and say 'Ah, you remind me of—' . . . well, whatever her name is. And sometimes they fall in love more deeply than before . . . with a girl I have given them."

16

It struck me that it had been a long while since I had heard the phrase "in love." How old-fashioned it sounded. "To fall in love" was out of style; the longing, the aching doubt, the heart-shivering hope, the trembling, innocent moment of avowal, all belong to another, older time . . .

And yet, I thought, Edward Granville's books were still read. And enough people wanted to know about him to make a biography worthwhile.

He turned back from the balustrade, and made a gesture of resignation. "One uses everything," he said. "And everything suffers a sea-change, a magicking."

Magicking; was there such a word? I doubted it; but I thought—foolishly—that I knew what he meant. "I understand," I said.

He gave me an odd look. "No, you do not, I think," he said. "But you will."

He led the way back into the house again, and shortly afterwards he said goodnight, and I went upstairs to my room, to work on my notes.

But I felt that I had missed something . . . that there was something in Granville's manner, or in the character of the man himself, that had eluded me—something I hadn't reached, some secret that had escaped me. That phrase, "a sea-change," . . . I tried to remember Ariel's song:

'Nothing of him but doth fade,
But doth suffer a sea-change
Into something rich and strange' . . .

Outside, the sound of silence hummed in my ears, until an owl hooted somewhere among the crags. This was not going to be an easy book to write; and it was quite a while before I got to sleep that night.

CHAPTER

2

There was fog along the coast when I awoke; downstairs, the ashes of last night's fire were gray in the fireplace, the house felt cold and damp, and all the sounds were hollow. There was no movement anywhere, no sign of the Mexican woman; I peered into the kitchen, but it looked dim and forbidding, and made me feel lonely. I got myself a glass of water, and lit a cigarette, and went through the living room out onto the terrace.

The terrace was wet, bare, and fog-shrouded, the sea below lost in the gray air. I hugged my jacket around me, feeling the cold on my face and in my bones. Somewhere along the coast a foghorn bellowed faintly, and more distant still, another faintly replied.

A girl came over the balustrade at one end of the terrace, and walked toward me. She was young and slender, dressed in a soft skirt and a cashmere sweater, a blue scarf over her hair. "Well, hello," she said, holding out her hand. "I'm sorry about the fog, but it will burn off after a bit."

For a moment I thought of the girl I had seen —or thought I had seen—on my way up the coast; the one who had turned into a tree. "I'm Michael Robb," I said.

She had a good face, with clean bones, and honest eyes. "I know," she said. "You're the one who's come to do Edward's . . . Mr. Granville's . . . life."

She looked up at the fog-shrouded house with its blank windows, and then looked back at me with a sympathetic expression. "No one's up, is there?" she said. "And you've had no breakfast."

I had no idea who she was. As far as I knew, Granville had no daughter—in fact, no relative of any kind. A neighbor, perhaps? She had called him Edward, so she must know him very well . . . or else she had known him for a long time. Was she his secretary, then? She didn't look like a secretary to me. Unless, of course . . .

"Let's go and see what there is in the kitchen," she said. "You must be starved."

For a neighbor, she seemed quite at home in the house; she seemed to know where everything was. She set water to boil on the stove, made coffee, found a cache of eggs in the refrigerator, and sliced up a loaf of bread for toast. "Do you often come by on a foggy morning?" I asked. She laughed, and shook her head. "Today Mr. Granville's housekeeper is off," she said.

"I'm afraid I came at a bad time," I said uncomfortably.

"Of course not," she assured me.

"Mrs. Granville's being away, too . . ."

She stopped buttering the toast for a moment, and gave me an oddly questioning look. "Yes," she declared. "She is."

I said that I had hoped to meet her. "Oh," she said lightly, "I've no doubt you will."

"Will she be back soon?"

"It all depends," she said.

On what? I wondered. But she didn't say, and I didn't think it was my business to ask. I didn't want to seem to pry.

Anyway, having her there in the kitchen with me changed the whole atmosphere of the house. It didn't feel cold and silent anymore; the breakfast-nook looked bright, and there was a warm odor of coffee and bacon in the air. There was another odor, too: the faint fragrance of the girl herself. I don't know what it was; it smelled like fresh, very delicate tea. She had taken off her scarf, and her hair, the color of wild honey, hung down around her shoulders. She couldn't have been more than twenty . . . a pretty girl, with a clear, clean look, and eyes the color of mountain skies.

"Do you know this country, Mr. Robb?" she asked.

I replied that I knew it only through the works of Robinson Jeffers. "A somber man," she said.

"He was like a gray day at sea, with a kind of fierceness held back. We were fond of him; I never knew if he liked me or not."

I asked her if her parents lived nearby. "They live in Salem," she said, "in Massachusetts. They've lived there all their lives."

I counted it out silently: Jeffers had died in '62, four years ago. She could have been sixteen. "We," she had said. She might have been at boarding school.

I didn't know why that seemed to make everything all right—except that it established her, so to speak, in time and space. I could see her as a schoolgirl visiting with her class the distinguished homes of the neighborhood, possibly on Garden Day . . . to sit shyly, full of awe and ignorance, in the livingrooms of the mighty.

She wanted to know what books I had written. I told her that I hadn't written any books, but that I had done a number of articles including one on the poetry of the 'twenties; at which she surprised me by quoting Elinor Wylie:

> *"The bird Imagination,*
> *That flies so far, that dies so soon;*
> *Her wings are colored like the sun,*
> *Her breast is colored like the moon.*
>
> *Weave her a chain of silver twist,*
> *And a little hood of scarlet wool,*
> *And let her perch upon your wrist,*
> *And tell her she is beautiful."*

"Did you know her?" she asked innocently. "She was so proud of her beauty."

I pointed out to her that I was a little young to have known Miss Wylie, who had died long ago. "Before you were born," I told her.

It was one thing for her to have known Jeffers; but to have her quote Wylie startled me. I was still thinking about it when Granville appeared, unshaven and in his dressing-gown. "I see that you two have met," he said; and seated himself between us.

I expected her to be surprised, or even shocked at his appearance, but apparently she was used to it, for she went, smiling, to get him his coffee and cook his eggs, and he turned amiably to me. "The years slip away," he said; "one tries to remember the past as it really was, but one remembers only a part of it. I had many friends, and most of them are dead; they left a legend behind them. We'd like to think that our youth was madder, brighter, happier than it was. It comforts us as we grow older, to believe that once upon a time we danced at dawn in a fountain. Few of us did, actually."

He sat silent a while, remembering. "As a matter of fact," he said at last, "we were a serious-minded generation; we thought the age best expressed by Dos Passos, rather than Fitzgerald. We were rebels; and embraced freedom; yet we committed ourselves to love, and we were hopeful. Of what, I cannot exactly say: perhaps of a better way of life on earth. Well, we had reason: the last trump was not as close then as it is to-day."

He smiled, a little sadly. "For us," he said, " *'the world stood out on either side'* . . ."

" *'No wider than the heart is wide,'* " the girl said. It was a quotation from Millay, from a time when Millay must have been at the same age as the girl herself . . . Granville might have known Millay; he might even have been one of her lovers. There must have been something in the way I looked at him which caused him to shake his head gently. "No," he said; "I never met her."

"And neither did . . ." he turned to the girl, and a look that was not so much a look as a moment of acceptance or understanding passed between them. "Neither did Nina," he said.

So her name was Nina. He didn't mention her last name, and I didn't ask. I had a feeling that he wanted me to accept the situation—whatever it was—without too many questions. Perhaps he liked a little scent of mystery around him.

"It was all so long ago," he said, "and so much has changed. Do you remember Whiteman's saxophones? . . . No, of course you don't. They made a lovely sound, full of longing. I remember the *Rhapsody In Blue* at Carnegie Hall, and the saxophones . . . It was an experience; a moment like the first kiss or hearing Caruso for the first time . . .

"They have rewritten the score for brass," he

said. "There is no wonder in the world any more. It is all over."

I saw him watching me, and I thought of my first flight in a plane, seeing the intense, blue, sunfilled sky face to face, and the sense of peace and clarity . . .

"I don't believe it," I said.

He glanced at the girl for a moment, and then he looked at me and smiled. "I'm glad," he said, as though I had passed a test of some kind. "I couldn't write, without wonder."

After breakfast he took me into his study to work. I had some questions I wanted to ask him about the early years, in particular his friendship with the poet Stephen Vincent Benét. "You have mentioned him in your novels," I said; "Tell me, what was he like?"

"He was a man of great honor," he said. "I loved him very much. He was a sorcerer; with his wife Rosemary, he created a world of enchantment. They married early, and their marriage was a love affair which lasted until his death, and beyond it. The only one I know of in our time."

"From what I have read there seem to have been a lot of sorcerers in those days," I said. "Magicians . . ."

He sighed, and shook his head. "The world has always been full of magicians," he said; "they crowd the bookstore shelves, they fill the theaters . . . . but they do not do anything with the heart, the way Benét did. They do tricks with cards, with a chicken in a hat . . . It is all sleight of hand, one can buy such tricks anywhere, even in a brothel. The true sorcerer deals with illusion; he does things with the heart."

I happened at that moment to glance outside, and saw Nina walking across the little patio among the flowering bushes. The fog was lifting, although the air was still gray, but there was a faint promise of sunshine later in the day. She went slowly along the stone path, and started up the hill behind the house.

"A wizard does things with the heart," said Granville.

The girl went to the top of the rise and stood there looking down. A breath of fog covered her for a moment, and when it had passed, she was gone. "She has turned into a tree," I said. I had not intended to say it; I had simply thought it, and must have said it anyway.

Edward Granville looked at me in surprise. "Why, no," he said matter-of-factly; "I am sure she has not done so."

CHAPTER

———

3

The fog had burned off by noon, as Nina had said it would. She was not with us at lunch, although the table was set—for two; and a green salad and a plate of cold meats laid out for us. Granville ate steadily, his thoughts apparently still in the past which my questions had revived for him. "A man is often remembered," he said musingly, "more for the way he lived—or died —than for what he wrote. Or else, he turns into his own creation: Cervantes becomes Quixote, Byron, Don Juan. And Hemingway the strong man without fear or pity, and Scott Fitzgerald forever young and beautiful."

"And damned?" I asked.

"Yes," he said. "But resurrected."

He went on to explain that every writer, upon his death, goes into limbo, there to wait for his work either to be brought to life again, or to be forgotten forever. "Some," he said, "raised up by their friends or by the scholars, enjoy a short second-life, but fall again into obscurity, and that is the true death from which there is no awakening. Others wait in their obscurity, and wait in vain, and fade at last into a note in an appendix. But some, like Shelley, shine more brightly than in their lifetimes.

"Naturally, there are exceptions. Goethe was never in eclipse; as a literary figure, he never died. He was worshipped in life, and still stands among the top immortals, august, revered, and anti-Semitic. One cannot speak with certainty about the Greeks or the Romans, for the Dark Ages intervened, when all knowledge was in the Church, and nothing was known for sure except that the earth was flat. As for today's candidates, it is still too soon to tell; and besides, there are too many . . . Each year the critics of the establishment pick out a new young man to wear the laurel, each with a name as unfamiliar to me as the one before. And last year's laureate fades into history, along with Whittier, and William Vaughn Moody."

That afternoon he spoke of his friends again, and of his wife. I was surprised to learn that they had been married for nearly thirty years; but taking into account his inaccessibility to the public, it was not after all strange that his private life should have remained obscure.

He went on to say that he realized that his work was no longer popular, and that it did not deserve to be. "As I told you," he said, "I create my own world; but it is a world of the past, it belongs to another time. After all—what other world do I know? It is filled with my friends, or those who would have been my friends; unlike the middle-aged young gentlemen of England, I am unable to look back in anger. I write about love; today's lovers probably wonder what I mean, for they themselves think of love as something quite different . . . less innocent, perhaps, less full of anguish. I believe the balance of the sexes has been disturbed, but I do not know how to weigh the disturbance. So, when I write about love, it is only about something I remember."

He seemed to enjoy talking, though I wasn't sure that he was actually talking to me, and not to some ghostly audience of his own.

"Yes," he said, "I remember. And for the artist to remember is to be in love again. It seems that to write, I must be in love; at my age that would appear to create something of a problem, would it not?"

I thought of the girl Nina. "I don't know," I said honestly.

"For the novelist," he said, "it is not too hard. All we have to do is turn our plain, ordinary sweethearts into beauties and ourselves into heroes—or into monstrous villains, depending on the popular taste."

"When did you ever follow the popular taste?" I asked.

He smiled—a little smugly, I thought. "When did I ever turn myself into a villain?" he asked.

"Never," I said. "No one ever thinks of you as a villain."

He nodded, and made a wry grimace. "Actually," he said, "a great many people think of me as dead; they think that I died years ago. They believe that my books are posthumous. On such few occasions as I have met a reader—always a lady—she has turned pale and scuttled away as soon as she decently could. One got the impression that she thought she was talking to Hawthorne or Washington Irving."

I never really knew if he was laughing at me. He gave me a solemn, melancholy look, followed all at once by a gleeful chuckle. "But I survived," he said. "Like Merlin, trapped in his tree by the nymph Nimue, I am still alive."

But then his mind seemed to slip off onto a new and other train of thought. "It is a fact," he said solemnly, "that in the insect world, the nymph is often deadlier than the adult. The dragonfly, for instance . . . There is a story in that, somewhere, I think . . ."

He thought about it for a moment or so before turning back to our conversation. "Where was I?" he asked.

"You were saying that you were still alive," I told him; "like Merlin."

"Well, there you are," he said vaguely; and seemed disinclined to continue the subject.

We worked until mid-afternoon, on Granville's early, eastern period, the years in Greenwich Village and later in Provincetown where he had met his wife. "She was working at the Wharf Theater," he said; "they were doing something by O'Neill—I've forgotten what. They were always doing something by O'Neill. She played an old woman."

"She was a young actress?"

"She was twenty-eight."

That meant that she was nearly sixty now. I hoped that she would return to Stonecliff from wherever she was in time for me to meet her; I wanted to get her to talk about her husband; I needed a woman's point of view for the book. Besides, I had a feeling that her return would somehow manage to place the girl Nina in her proper frame, whatever that was: probably that of a young admirer, a "fan", a pretty girl sitting worshipfully at an old man's knee.

A little before four, Granville announced that he had worked long enough and that he intended to retire to his bedroom for a nap. The day was still bright, the slopes above the house washed in clear afternoon light, and I decided to walk for a while on those slopes, among the trees, following the path taken earlier by Nina.

The sea stretched away below me, blue-dark to the horizon, the shining sky floated above my head. All was silent. It was not an empty silence, but rather a waiting stillness in which life was

not so much absent as watching and listening
. . . for some word to be spoken, for some moment to occur.

I thought about what Granville had said about
the continuing act of creation. "To conceive of
God at all," he had said, "we must first accept the
fact with Aquinas that He is inconceivable.
Those were not the Good Doctor's exact words,
but they express his meaning. 'We cannot know
what God is,' is what he said. Or, as Karl Barth
points out, any search for God that starts with
human experience is in vain. The reason for this
can be expressed in the form of an equation: If
the universe is incomprehensible, the He-or-It
who created it must be more incomprehensible
still. Man is a three-dimensional creature: Time,
Eternity, Infinity—the fourth, fifth, and sixth
dimensions are merely words to him, he does not
comprehend them in the sense that he compre-
hends the roundness of a ball or the measure-
ments of a cube. A caterpillar going round and
round the rim of an earthenware pot in the garden has no knowledge of where it is, or what a
pot might be, or even of the meaning of a garden; how much less, then, can it imagine—or
hope to comprehend—the man who created that
garden and placed the pot in it! When it comes to
understanding where we are, what our planet
may be, what a universe is—and Who is behind
it all—we are as much in the dark as the caterpillar. How absurd, then, to speak of God as being dead—or, for that matter, alive; those are

mortal words, and have no meaning outside our own dimension."

Rounding an outcrop of rock, the path led down a short slope toward a small grove of trees in the middle of which, cradled in the lower branches of an old, gnarled oak, I saw a little house—a tree-house, such as a father might have built for his children. It was empty; there was no one in it—or so I thought. I peered inside, and saw, in the dusty, leafy gloom, what I took to be a coil of tarred rope . . . until it lifted its head, uncoiled, and slid away across the floor, flicking its forked tongue as it went.

For some reason I thought of Merlin, immured in his tree by Nimue long ago.

CHAPTER

4

Nina was with us again at supper, in a dress which struck me as old-fashioned. I am no expert in women's clothes; it might have been the way she wore it, or even something in the girl herself that seemed to belong to an older, more feminine period.

She wanted to know how the day's work had gone, and Granville declared himself satisfied with our progress. "It is very difficult to talk about oneself," he declared, "without saying either too much or too little. If too little, one appears more humble than one is; and if too much, the effect is apt to be confused."

"Mr. Granville talked mostly about his friends," I said. "And about his wife."

I threw this last remark out as negligently as I could, watching to see what effect, if any, it would have on her. If I expected her to blush,

or fidget, I was disappointed, for she looked inter-
ested and on the whole, I thought, pleased. "Oh?"
she asked. "What did he say about her?"

She seemed almost childishly eager to be told,
and Granville laughed. "Let's not discuss the absent," he said; but I thought I heard a note of dis-
approval in his voice.

She looked down at her plate, and it seemed to
me that her cheeks had turned a little pink, and
her eyes—(possibly? or was it the candle-light?)
—a trifle moist. Well, I thought, I have touched
her; but whether with a scratch or a deadly
wound, I didn't know. A glance at Granville himself told me nothing; he continued to eat placidly,
unconcerned as before.

I remember thinking it odd at the time that he
didn't ask Nina what she had been doing with
herself all day, that he appeared to have no curi-
osity about her—although, knowing what I do
now, it was of course not strange at all. And yet
—how much *do* I know? Only the face of the
puzzle; only enough to ask questions for which
there are no simple or easy answers.

Nina served us, so naturally and unobtru-
sively that when I realized that she must also have
prepared the meal, I was not surprised. She had
cooked tender abalone steaks in a mushroom
sauce, with new potatoes in their skins, and the
first fresh green beans of the season; and Granville had opened a bottle of Sancerre. "I am not
one of those," he said, "who insist that our wines
are the equal of the French. I admit, it is often

hard to tell one from the other nowadays, but that is only because the French wines have deteriorated to such an extent—whether as a result of poor viniculture, wretched bottling, or the long journey westward, I am not prepared to say. The wines with which I compare our own pinots and sauvignons are those of long ago, and all gone by, yet I remember them very well. I assure you that nothing we bottle today is anything like them at all."

I saw that Nina was looking at him with a curiously intent expression. "That was before the War," she said. "You were in France with those wines."

He looked up at her for a moment, and then quietly pushed his glass aside. "Yes, I was," he said. "I was with Virginia."

She turned away, and I thought I heard her catch her breath. "I know," she said.

"There are no good cigars any more, either," he said, and sighed heavily.

I remarked that I had seen Merlin's house that afternoon.

"Merlin's house?" asked Nina.

"Merlin," I said; "the Druid. In a tree, up on a hill in back."

"Oh," she said; "the old tree-house." I looked over at Granville. "Was it ever used?" I asked. "For anything?"

"Of course," he said. And he added simply, "Have you ever made love in a tree?"

"Why no," I said; "I haven't." I felt embarrassed for the girl, and tried not to look at her.

"There are many beautiful places to make love in," he declared. "A tree-house is one of them. So is a garden in Florence, full of nightingales."

He was silent for a moment; we were all three of us silent. "There are no beautiful places left any more," he said at last.

"Well," I said, "there's the tree-house. But it had a snake in it."

Granville looked at me calmly. "Are you sure?" he asked. "Perhaps you imagined it."

And turning to Nina, he declared,

"Our young friend has a way of seeing things. He thought you had turned into a tree."

She gave a clear, silvery laugh. "What fun," she cried gaily; "if I had only thought of it!"

It was at this moment that it occurred to me for the first time that I might fall in love with her. I didn't put it to myself that simply; I only knew that I felt a sudden gaiety and delight, a moment at the threshold of happiness. I thought of us— of Nina and myself—in a tree-house. It was suddenly very exciting to think of her.

But I was troubled: what was Edward Granville to Nina? and what was she to him? It seemed impossible for me to ask, now that I knew my own feelings to be involved.

But were they really? I told myself that I scarcely knew the girl, that I had been with her only twice, at breakfast, and now at dinner. I didn't even know who she was, or where she came from; I didn't know her last name.

It was true that she was young, and pretty, and that she had a lovely way of laughing.

"But I didn't imagine the snake," I said. I felt obstinate about it, as though in some way I were being made to take part in an illusion.

Granville made a gesture with his cigar, deprecating and at the same time dismissive. "I didn't say you had imagined it," he declared; "what I meant was that you thought you saw it—which is not the same thing at all. To think you see something doesn't prove that it is there. Men have been known to die for an ideal which in a single season has proved false; men have fallen in love only to learn too late that what they thought they saw wasn't there at all."

I had to admit that he had a point, having thought myself in love more than once. Perhaps what I saw in Nina wasn't there, either.

That night the fog bank stood off the coast, held out at sea, and the terrace was in moonlight. The three of us stood together gazing out across the empty, moonlit void, hearing and smelling the sea, and breathing in the fragrance of the night-blooming jasmine, and the night-odor of roses. A star fell as we watched, streaking across the sky and vanishing; and Granville remarked,

"I am convinced that there are other beings in the universe besides ourselves."

He continued:

"I am not sure that they have not already visited us. The so-called flying saucer is not new: Ezekiel saw fiery wheels in the sky, one within the other, and each one a living creature. But whether they are here for good or ill, nobody knows."

He stared for a moment at the glowing tip of his cigar. "Perhaps," he said, "like the gods, they have come to make us mad."

Looking out to sea, it seemed to me that the fog bank had come closer.

"I am an old man," he said. "Fortunately I shan't be around when the time comes for them to eat us."

I felt rather than saw Nina stiffen at his side. "Oh hush!" she cried. "I wish you wouldn't talk like that. Besides . . . how do you know they aren't here to bless us?"

He looked at her enigmatically. "Do you feel blessed?" he asked, a little sadly, I thought.

"Yes," she said defiantly.

"Thank you," he said gravely.

Shortly after that he went back into the house and left the two of us together on the terrace. I felt uncomfortable, and uncertain; I wanted to say something to bridge the distance between us, the distance of two young people, strangers, on a moonlight night, with the odor of jasmine around them; but I couldn't think of any way to reach her, except through Granville. "He is not at all the way I expected," I said.

The moonlight made shadows on her face as she turned to look at me. "What did you expect?" she asked. "What did you think he would be like?"

"Like his books," I said. "The way other writers are."

"Are they?" she said. "I wonder." And she added firmly,

"He is more like his books than you think."

"But they are love stories!" I exclaimed.

"Yes," she said. "And he has lived them all. That's why they seem so real. He lives in his books."

I don't know what got into me: the moonlight, perhaps, or the jasmine, or the far-off, half-heard murmur of the sea. "What about you?" I asked. "Do you live in his books too?"

I expected her to freeze, or to turn away in anger; and thought, too late, that I had been unforgivably impertinent. But to my surprise, she turned to me with kindness. It was as though I had comforted her.

"Yes," she said.

I noticed Granville's face when we returned to the house. He seemed displeased; was it because we had been out there too long together, Nina and I?

CHAPTER

5

I told myself that she hadn't understood my meaning—or that I had failed to understand hers. The thought that she might actually be involved in one of Granville's stories—that she might be living in it with him—struck me as unlikely as it was disagreeable. She was too young, he was a married man whose wife was returning almost any day; and besides, there was no sign of those starry, touched, and dreamy looks which are associated with young ladies in love. That she had affection for him was obvious, but it seemed to me almost wifely; whatever she felt for him, it wasn't what she could feel—must feel—for someone closer to her own age.

I had gone up to my room early, leaving them both downstairs in the study; I presumed that she had left soon afterwards. Even when I woke from my first sleep, thinking I heard footsteps in the hall outside, very light, very soft, moving toward Granville's room, I didn't think very much about it. But for some reason, I lay awake a long time (waiting for them to return?)—long enough to see the light turn gray in my window, and to hear the first morning sounds, the voices of doves in the garden.

The Mexican woman was in the kitchen when I came down, and breakfast was served to me in the breakfast nook. The day was clear and bright, the sea shining in the sun, but I had no appetite. There was a different kind of loneliness sitting there by myself, from anything I had felt before.

Granville didn't come down to breakfast, and when I finally joined him in the study, he appeared weary. However, he greeted me, if not eagerly, at least courteously, asked me how I had slept; and after a few remarks about the weather and the morning news which he had heard broadcast over his small bedside radio, we settled down to work.

I asked the usual questions about his methods of work; did he use a typewriter? did he dictate to a secretary? It turned out that he wrote in longhand, and in pencil. "I have never felt the need of a secretary," he said. "My wife types the finished manuscript for me, and edits as she goes. She is an excellent critic."

"I see," I said. So whatever else Nina was to him, she was not a secretary. In some ways it made things better, in others, worse. I didn't know how I felt about it.

I asked him about work-in-progress, and he told me that he had started a new novel, the story of a painter and a waif, a young girl. "The trouble is," he said, "I can't for the life of me make out how it's going to end. Usually my characters make that decision for me; I set them down as well as I can in flesh and blood, and they take over, drawn by their own natures to their destiny. Unfortunately, so far, they haven't given me any clear indication as to how things are going. He is in love with her, and would like to marry her, but perhaps he is too old. She has not made up her mind."

"Do you mean you're going to let the girl decide?" I asked.

"Naturally," he said. "She is a woman, and would resent having her mind made up for her."

"Let me see," I said; "you have written thirty novels . . ."

"Thirty-one . . . but no matter."

"Thirty-one, then. Do you find it harder as you go on?"

"Being mortal," he said, "I grow older. It is one of the conditions of life in this dimension that it should have a beginning and an end. The limbs grow less supple, the muscles stringier, the bones calcify, freshness leaves the spirit, the sense of wonder is harder to come by. And yet, at each beginning, I walk as before, like God in Eden in the cool of the day."

He sighed. "It's such a lovely moment," he said. "I'm happy then, for a while. Everything is bathed in a heavenly light. I haven't yet come upon the troubles involved in sending Adam and Eve out into the world."

There are only certain questions a biographer can ask, questions of fact and opinion. Out of them he must somehow get the full measure of a man. I had a feeling that I was failing in this; that the Edward Granville who answered my questions, who talked to me about his work and his friends, was in reality only a covering for a far more secret and shadowy self that rested and waited inside . . . like a wild animal lying quietly in its cage, with the mystery of another world behind its eyes. To what extent Granville was conscious of, and himself responsible for, this effect, I didn't know; the simple fact is that no one is ever wholly open to anyone else.

As the morning wore on, I found myself growing more and more restless, and impatient. For I realized that the person I really wanted to see was Nina. But it was already late afternoon, and Granville had retired as usual for his nap, before I saw her. She had not appeared at lunch; and it was only by chance, walking along the path from the house to the road, that I caught a glimpse of her seated cross-legged in a patch of sweet-grass with her back to a rock warmed by the sun.

I asked if I might join her, and she patted the ground next to her. "Tell me," she said, as I let myself down at her side, "how is the work going?"

"I don't know," I answered truthfully. I told her that Mr. Granville was something of an enigma to me. "I don't quite know where I am with him," I said. "I gather facts; we talk about God and the heavens; I know a good deal about his friends; but I haven't yet touched the true man—the man who lies in back of the waif and the painter . . ."

She turned to me quickly. "Then he has told you about Max?" she asked eagerly.

"Max?" I repeated stupidly.

"The painter," she said. "His name is Max. I thought you knew."

She seemed disappointed. "I thought perhaps he had talked to you about the new novel," she explained. "You see—when he can talk about it, that means that . . . well . . . it's not a false start. It means that he is really into it."

Apparently she had been through more than one novel with him. "He didn't say very much about it," I told her. "As a matter of fact, Mr. Granville was tired today. He was up late last night."

I suddenly remembered the footsteps in the hall. "I heard him on his way to bed," I said. "It was very late."

I watched her fingers plucking at the grass. "At least," I said, "I thought it was he."

There was something in the way she kept her head turned away from me that gave me a queer feeling in the pit of my stomach. Please, I thought, it *had* to be Granville. It *was* he, wasn't it?

"He often works late," she said at last.

She turned back to me with her usual direct, untroubled look. "Are you enjoying your stay at Stonecliff, Mr. Robb?" she asked.

Something got into me, then; perhaps it was her being so untouched. I wanted to reach her, touch her, make her answer me. "Yes," I said deliberately; "as long as you are here."

I saw her eyes widen with surprise before she turned away. She made a little, helpless gesture with her hands, and shook her head, more to herself than to me. It was as though a wall were suddenly there between us, a wall which had not been there before, but which she had known about, and yet had run into and been surprised.

It was the wrong thing for me to have said, and I realized it too late. "I'm sorry," I told her, "but I don't know how else to answer you. I've been working mostly; and that has been interesting enough. But whether I'm having joy, exactly . . ."

I laced my fingers around my knees, and leaned back. "I don't know," I said.

I looked around at the enormous panorama of ocean and sky, the sea-gray cliffs and dusty slopes crowned with the darker green of the cypress. The great headlands swept away on either side, to north and south, clear and hard in the north, hazy with sun in the south. "It's lovely here," I said, "but it's empty. One should be old and married—or young and in love, to live here, to be happy here. It's lonesome country otherwise . . ."

And I quoted from one of Granville's poems:

This is the country of the hungry heart.
This is the country where the noonday weather,
The scent of lilacs, or the summer night,
Can set us dreaming. We're a restless people,
We have a kind of distance in our eyes.

She took it up, dreamily—

A man can stop along a middling rise
And see the hills stand up across the land
Range after range, like shadows in the wind,
Dark on the pine and dusty on the heather.
They draw the heart, the air is full of light.
There is a beauty in American skies.

She smiled at me, and I reached for her hand, and finished the poem for her:

Somewhere among these hills he has a friend,
Somewhere my love and I will meet together.

She looked at me for a long while, and I thought that her eyes filled with tears, but she didn't cry. She drew her hand away at last, and shook her head again, just as she had done before.

"It isn't fair," she said.

I asked her what she meant, but she didn't answer; and after a while we walked back to the house together in silence.

47

CHAPTER

6

"I have been thinking," said Granville at dinner that night, "about the Jews. They never thought that their God was dead. Unlike all other ancient tribes and nations, when they were defeated in battle, their temples destroyed and their cities laid waste, they blamed only themselves. They believed that because of their sins God had turned away from them for the time being. Such obstinacy is all the more mysterious when one considers that it led to Christianity, to Augustine and Luther, Torquemada and Hitler."

"I'm not sure that I follow you," I said.

"If they had thought their God defeated," said Granville, "they would have become Baby-lonians in 586 B.C., and Romans in 70 A.D. And today they would be Arabs, Italians, Parisians, Prussians, and members of the Jonathan Club of Los Angeles."

"Then you don't think that Christianity was inevitable in any case?"

"Jesus was born in Judea," Granville replied, "and nowhere else. He could not have been an Assyrian, or Paul a Scythian. We have here a grand design to which we cannot be indifferent. At the same time it would be a mistake to think that this was all there is to it; there are still many mysteries which have yet to be explained. The megaliths of Stonehenge, set out with astonishing precision, are witnesses to a very ancient wisdom and mysterious powers. There was magic in the world long before God spoke to Abraham."

"He spoke to Adam first," I reminded him. "And then to Noah."

Granville studied me reflectively. "But not," he said, "surely not—in Hebrew?"

He sighed gustily. "The world does not change as much as we would like to think," he said. "I should not be in the least surprised to learn that a civilization very much like ours flourished several hundred million years ago, before the dinosaurs—lasted as long as our own, and ended in disaster as ours will."

He looked across the table. "And then we shall have the dinosaurs again," he said. "Or sixty-foot cockroaches, or armoured flies as big as a house. Already there are reports from New Mexico of jack-rabbits exposed to gamma rays which have increased enormously in size and ferocity."

"Then you don't think it will be the flying saucers that eat us?" I asked.

"They will eat us," he said, "if they find us edible. What puzzles me is their inability—or unwillingness—to communicate; although we do not communicate with our food, either. It may be that they do not make sounds, as we do, but communicate by means of radar, like the ants and other insects; or, again, they may 'scan' us by means of ESP, and finding us at heart ignorant, savage, fearful, and cruel, decide that we are indigestible."

He paused a moment. "On the other hand," he said slowly, "these visitors may be from our own world."

"From this planet Earth?"

"From a far distant future, when man has learned to break the time barrier."

"But wouldn't such men speak to us?"

"Travelling at the speed of light, they might be unable to. Or they might be very small men, and physically weak. Or they might not know where they were—or when; and hesitate to approach us, just as we would hesitate to set down in a nest of Neanderthal. We think of early Stone Age men as being giants, like Gog and Magog —not realizing that we ourselves tower over our ancestors. We do not have their strength, of course."

He seemed to be in a more expansive mood than usual; his conversation always rolled grandly, but on this occasion more grandly still

. . . almost as though he were asking—plead-ing—for attention. From whom? I had been watching Nina; she seemed both present and far away, her thoughts withdrawn behind her face; and yet, in an absent way, presiding at table like the lady of the house . . . which, in the ab-sence of Virginia Granville, I was obliged to realize she was.

It was an uncomfortable thought. And sud-denly something that Granville had said before came to mind: the wizard deals in illusion, he does things with the heart. Had he enchanted her? She sat there as though in a spell, relaxed and dreamy; she had too much poise for her age.

He had said a wizard, as opposed to a mere magician. A magician used tricks, but a wizard was a sorcerer, an enchanter; he caused things to appear as other than they were, he made you see things the way he wanted you to see them.

But did he want me to see Nina as the lady of the house? Then how was I to think of Virginia Granville, absent—conveniently?

The Mexican woman served us, as usual in si-lence; whatever her thoughts were, they were hidden behind the mask of her face. No one asked her anything—as I would be asked when I left Stonecliff, and expected by the world to reply. Besides—she couldn't feel—how could she?— that sudden focusing of the heart's attention (was it some sort of anguish, like a tiny blow?) when-ever she looked at Nina.

"Yes," Granville was saying, "the giants of

the past often became smaller in review. When Victor Hugo died, he was given a state funeral, and an entire nation mourned; but today we think more often of Stendhal. My own parents admired the works of Chesterton, Galsworthy, and Arnold Bennett; they thought them as solid as the society they mirrored. Today they slumber undisturbed in the ruins of an empire. So many of my own friends sleep unremembered too—as I shall sleep some day."

"Perhaps," said Nina in a cool, small voice, "Mr. Robb would care to tell us something about himself for a change."

Arrested in full cry, Granville was left, so to speak, with his mouth open. "Why, yes," he managed to say at last; "I have probably been talking too much.

"Tell us about yourself, Michael."

What could I tell them, I wondered? My father was in real estate in Minnesota, my mother taught school in Little Falls. I was an only child . . . how could that interest them? "I took my Master's at Stanford," I said. "I write articles for the magazines . . . I did a piece on Leonard Wibberley for *Holiday*. That's what gave your publishers the idea . . ."

"I knew Leonard in his San Raphael days," said Granville. "You must let me see it."

"I write a little poetry," I said. "I live in the San Fernando Valley, and barbecue steaks for my friends . . ."

I could feel myself faltering; how ordinary I

52

sounded! But what else was there to say? Could I tell them what it was like to live alone in a city, with my hopes and a typewriter? Granville would have known all that himself, from his own youth—and Nina wouldn't have understood it. Could I tell them how, in the dim blue California evenings I dreamed of doing great and beautiful things? How music moved me? sitting in the summer night in the cold, dark hollow of the Hollywood hills . . . ?

"I hope some day to write a novel of my own," I said diffidently.

"Tst!" said Granville. "I feel sorry for you."

"Why?" I asked lightly. "I'd like, for once, to fall in love with someone of my own. I've never read Bennett, or Chesterton—but I've been in love with more than one young woman out of Mr. Granville's books."

I had been talking, really, to Nina all the time, and watching her; and when I spoke of having been in love with some of Granville's heroines, I saw her throw a quick look across the table at him. It was a strange look, in which I thought I saw—for the fraction of a second that it lasted—both appeal and condemnation. But he was looking away, and whatever it was, he didn't seem to see it.

"You ought at least to read Chesterton," he remarked; and quoted:

" 'Love-light of Spain—hurrah!
Death-light of Africa!

Don John of Austria
Is riding to the sea.' "

"That's understandable, at any rate!"

I scarcely heard him. I was thinking about the way Nina had spoken to him, and how he had meekly changed the subject. It was not at all the way I would have expected a young person to talk to a distinguished author.

After dinner, Granville took his cigar out onto the terrace, a thing, he assured me, he never used to do before the Cuban revolution. "A good cigar," he said, "should be smoked indoors only; but what I am able to get today, does just as well in the garden."

Nina, for once, did not accompany him, preferring to stay indoors near the fire; and I found an excuse to stay with her. She seemed ill-at-ease, complained of feeling chilly, and drew a soft woolen scarf around her shoulders. "I'm afraid I lied a bit," I said. "As a matter of fact I know a little Chesterton, besides *Lepanto*."

I quoted:

'The gallows in my garden, people say,
Is new and neat and adequately tall . . . '

She laughed, and finished the stanza:

'The strangest whim has seized me . . .
After all I think I will not hang myself today.'

"How mischievous of you," she said, "to pretend ignorance."

It struck me as a curiously old-fashioned remark for a young girl to make; and in fact, for a moment, standing there warming her fingers at the fire and with the shawl across her shoulders, she gave the impression of a much older woman. But when she caught me watching her, her expression changed; her lips tilted up, her eyes darkened, and suddenly she was a young girl again.

I thought of how she had interrupted Granville at dinner. "I was surprised at the way you spoke to him," I said.

She flushed, and bit her lip. "It was a mistake," she said. "For a moment, I forgot."

I wondered what it was that she forgot; his age? or her own? "Well," I said, "you now know all there is to know about me, and I know almost nothing about you."

Again I thought how grown-up she looked, her lips set in a prim line, the firm, delicate chin held high. "I never talk about myself," she said.

"You told me that your parents live in Salem," I reminded her. "That much, at least."

"Well, they do," she said defiantly.

"Do they know what you are doing?"

"Yes," she said, "they have known it for a long time." But her eyes wavered, and she looked away.

The fact was, I didn't know what she was doing, myself. I couldn't ask her, outright: what are you and Granville to each other? Not yet, at any rate; though I certainly intended to some day.

And I didn't know how she felt about me, either. I believed that I troubled her, and that pleased me—because to trouble a girl is the first step; but I felt, too, that she didn't want to be troubled, didn't want it at all, and would resist it; and that she even had, in some way unknown to me, the strength to say No, no matter what.

Unless she was in love, she ought not to have that strength. And yet, I couldn't believe that she was Granville's mistress. I rejected it absolutely.

Granville was returning from the terrace, and I spoke to her quickly. "Can I see you home to-night?" I asked.

"No," she said.

I must have looked the way I felt, for she made a sudden helpless gesture of resignation.

"I live here," she said simply.

CHAPTER

7

There were no footsteps in the hall that night; I was left alone with my uncertain thoughts. Somewhere in the house, Nina lay sleeping; was she alone, like myself? I could not think of her in any other way. Whatever she was doing in Stonecliff, whatever her situation in the household, I had to believe that she was not in bed with Granville.

Soft sounds at night, secret noises, have a way of penetrating sleep. I could have slumbered on through a thunderstorm—but some time after midnight, I was awakened by a sound beneath my window, a light sound, so faint, in fact, that I wondered why it had awakened me at all, and yet it brought me out of bed and to the window.

It was a clear night, black and still. A faint glow around the corner of the house from the direction of the patio made me realize that lights were on in Granville's study; apparently he was still at work. For a moment, I couldn't imagine what I had heard. And then, darker even than the night, the monstrous shape of a cougar swam out of the blackness below, padded silently across the faint patch of light, and disappeared in the darkness beyond.

Night, sleep, and waking sometimes play queer tricks. I stood at the window, wondering what to do; wondering, too, if I had really seen what I thought I had seen. Ought I to warn Granville? I remembered the snake in the tree-house; perhaps he would dismiss this, too, as something I had imagined.

In the end I decided to go back to bed again, and to deal with it—reality or dream—in the morning.

But in the morning I decided not to mention it. For one thing, a quick but careful scrutiny of the ground beneath my window showed no trace of any animal having passed that way during the night; there were no prints of pads or paws, no bent or broken branches, no spoor. And for another, Nina at breakfast appeared reserved and distant, replying to my few attempts at conversation with monosyllables, which gave me something else to worry about.

Granville, too, was in a thoughtful mood when I joined him in the study. "When Christianity first came to Britain," he remarked, "it must have seemed a fearsome thing to the Druids. To replace their Corn God with the Trinity—what an incredible proposal! Particularly since the Corn God was several thousand years old, and Jesus less than four hundred."

"Surely you are not involved in the troubles of the Fourth Century!" I exclaimed.

"I am involved in those of the Twentieth," said Granville. He continued:

"We are in a period of ferment not unlike that the Middle Ages, when the students also rioted in the universities. Then, as now, they became a force to be reckoned with. It was a force for better things, a longing for light, after the Dark Ages. It gave us the great cathedrals, and led to the Renaissance. What the present ferment will lead to, I do not know."

"Sir," I said, politely but earnestly, "what the young people want today is freedom. The freedom of the individual conscience."

"Yes," he said patiently; "I know. But when everyone is Luther, what happens to the individual conscience? It is lost in conformity."

And he hummed a line from *The Gondoliers*:

" 'When everyone is somebody, Then no one's anybody.'

"We, too," he said, "blamed our parents for the sorry state of the world."

He sighed. "Still," he added, "I do not delude myself into thinking that the world can return to the past. Those days are over; there have been convulsions, and things have changed—one hopes for the better. I only wish that what is to come will not be ugly."

"Life is ugly," I said; but I spoke without conviction, and he was quick to catch it. "You don't really believe that," he said.

"A lot of people do," I said doggedly. "And there's a lot of ugliness in the world."

"There is indeed," he agreed; "but ugliness is not the only reality. There are other things besides. Why should we be greatly obliged to the artist for telling us that slime is brown, and snot is green? It only spoils our appetite for lunch. History is full of anguish: there was never a time when people weren't being put to the sword or the torch, or dying of the plague or the weather. And yet—who remembers the slaughter of the Amalekites?"

"The Amalekites?"

"You see! You don't know who they are. They furnished David with something to sing about. All we remember are the Psalms."

"The Amalekites remember," I said.

He gave me a wintry smile. "There are no Amalekites left," he said. "And I am the last of the Druids."

We worked until noon, Granville doing the talking and I taking notes, and then went to lunch which the Mexican woman served on the terrace. Nina was nowhere to be seen, and in her absence Granville asked me if I would mind driving him into Los Olivos where he had some business to attend to.

I took my car, and we drove slowly along the corniche, enjoying the clear, sun-glinting air, the sparkling sea far below. I wanted very much to talk about Nina, and cast about for some way to begin.

To my surprise, it was Granville who mentioned her first. "Nina," he began, and stopped.

I murmured something complimentary, to which he made no reply. "She told me that her parents live in the east," I said. "Who are they?"

"Their name is Kneeland."

Kneeland . . . Kneeland; the name stirred a vague memory. It seemed to me that there had been a Miss Kneeland married years ago to someone in the news—a French count? a bullfighter? an opera singer? Hemingway? No, not Hemingway. I gave it up; it had all happened before my time; and in any case, it was not my concern; it belonged to another period; it was of no importance any more.

"Salem was where they burned the witches," I said.

"They burned a few frightened old women," said Granville, "and one young one. Her beauty went up in smoke, along with her dreams. Nina has been more fortunate."

"At least," I said lightly, "she has kept her beauty."

He gave me a strange look. "Why, yes," he said slowly; "she has kept her beauty."

"And her dreams?" I asked innocently.

"I would like to think so," he answered gravely.

I felt a quick curdle of jealousy at his tone,

which was that of a proprietor; was he warning me against trespassing? Yet there was something else, something more: for I realized that I was jealous of the man himself. I was jealous of what he was, jealous of his place in the world, even though that place was no longer in the sun—of his work, his many years, his knowledge, and a certain manner that came perhaps not so much from serenity as from acceptance—the acceptance of his disappointments and failures, as well as whatever true things he had accomplished; secure, at least, in that. I was jealous, actually, of age itself, of the long years piled one upon another, the great things seen, the disasters averted or outlived, the loves known and remembered, the full life—the monument.

"Dreams," he said. "But they, too, are illusions; or haven't you learned that yet?"

"Perhaps mine are," I said. "I wouldn't want hers to be."

He seemed scarcely to have heard me. "Youth too," he declared. "Illusion."

He sighed, and laid a rough, dry hand on mine for a moment. "She is not what you think," he said.

It was curiously comforting, although I didn't know if it were meant to be. The heavy load on my spirit lifted, and was replaced by a feeling of excitement and anticipation—of what, I didn't know, either. I was young, Nina was young, and she was not Granville's mistress . . . Surely, that was what he meant? Else why say that she was not what I thought? He must have known that it was not so much what I thought, as what I feared.

"I used to be a fencer," he was saying; "my weapon was the saber. Of course, that was a long time ago. I was never very great, but I learned something: you think the blade is there, but in the hands of a wizard it is always somewhere else."

"Then for someone facing a wizard," I said, "that is a very important thing to know."

"The blow," he said, "comes from an unexpected quarter."

We did our business in the town, stopping off at the bank, the stationery store, the library, and the bakery; after which we started home again. The sun was low, shining in our eyes; as we turned inland at one point, among the taller trunks of the sequoias, it fell like a golden dust between the trees, making a pattern of light and shade in which shapes seemed to form and melt and form again in shadowy design of leaf and fern, bush and boulder.

Granville was silent most of the way, and little by little I felt the well-being drain out of me and uneasiness set in. "The blow," he had said, "comes from an unexpected quarter." I wondered once again if he was warning me, trying to tell me something.

He broke his own silence at last. "Tell me, Michael," he said, "shall you be with us at Stonecliff much longer? It is not that I find our conversations anything but agreeable—being as they are about me—but it's time I got back to more serious things . . . to my book again.

"Not that you haven't been of help to me even there," he added quickly, "though not in the way I had expected."

"It must be very difficult for you," I said. "But can you spare me just a few more days? It would be very useful to me."

And I added: "If I could wait until Mrs. Granville gets back . . ."

He raised his hand to stop me. "That would be impossible, I'm afraid," he said.

"But I thought . . ." I began . . .

I never finished the sentence; instead, I had to wrench at the steering wheel to keep the car from going off the road. Because, as we turned toward the coast again, coming out of the big trees, among the rocks and the junipers in the slanting, dusty light, I saw—or thought I saw—a great, tawny shape among the thinning trees, among the shadows; and at its side, with her hand on its head, Nina.

I saw them—if I saw them—only for a moment. But in that moment I had let the car stray. They vanished among the trees; and I brought us back to the right side of the road again, and turned, confused and apologetic, to my companion.

Edward Granville sat erect in his seat, a faint smile on his face, his gaze intent and fixed on something in front of him as invisible as the air.

His right wrist and hand were making small, swift movements, as though he were conducting a symphony; as though he had a baton in his hand—or a saber.

CHAPTER

8

It was the next day that brought me closer to Granville's world and drew me deeper into the shadows of illusion.

I had been given the afternoon off from work, as Granville had said that he wished to be alone; and I was walking in the woods on the slopes above Stonecliff, when I came, as before, on the tree with the tree-house in its branches. But this time the tree-house was not empty, for Granville was sitting in the doorway, talking to someone. I couldn't see who it was, because of the leaves, but trees and leaves also screened me from sight, and I was able to listen to the conversation.

I heard a man's voice declare: "The mountain lion is here." The voice was sad, and elderly.

"I know," Granville replied. "It is too soon. I am not ready for him."

"You will have to decide what to do," said the

other; "you must make up your mind how things are to turn out. I have enough problems as it is."

"I am not aware of them," said Granville coldly. "What problems do you have, except the girl?"

The other, whoever he was, gave an aggrieved exclamation. "Do you think there are no problems for a painter," he asked, "except being in love?"

"I don't know what they are," said Granville.

"Then learn," said the other. "For one thing, what kind of painter am I? We have had primitives before, from Cimabue to Rousseau; they were innocent and naïve. Today's primitives are not so innocent. Shall I paint abstractions? It is very hard to tell people how to look at a thought; they can only look at it with another thought.

"You will have to make up your mind."

"Paint the evening air," said Granville moodily. "Paint what you see."

"Figures tell you nothing," said the other. "From a nude without a head you get no information."

"Then paint young people's faces," said Granville.

"Do you know this world of young people?" asked the other. It was clear to me that he did not think so.

"Perhaps not," said Granville uncomfortably. "I don't know. I am trying to learn. And I have help, of a sort."

"That, too, is an illusion."

"I know," said Granville in a low voice.

"Let me tell you about it," said the other. "The faces of young people today are closed and secret; they do not like us. It is not at all the way it was in Paris. Do you remember the Butte? the streets at dawn, the morning smells, the white dome of Sacre Coeur high above the city, and the sky of spring, tender and shining with its gentle clouds low in the south over the Tourraine? In those days, to be young, in Paris, was to be happy even when things were sad. And love had a glow, a tenderness . . . it gave people joy.

"This feeling I have gives me no joy. Let me off, Edward; allow me to give it up. This girl you have chosen for me is too young; she is in love with youth, not with me. When she looks at me, it is without force, without any wounds; do you understand me? the air between us is like sunlight, there is no anguish in it . . . except for me. Nothing can come of it, but sorrow. I didn't ask you for that."

"You didn't ask me for anything," said Granville. "But I gave you all I had."

"Then find something else for me."

There was silence for a moment; then Granville said harshly: "Would you rather be alone in the world?"

"No—no; that would be terrifying. But give me someone nearer my own age."

"I'll think about it," said Granville; but I could tell from his tone that he was upset. "I wanted

you to love Halys," he said. I heard him strike
the bare boards of the platform with his knuckles.
"By God," he exclaimed, "and so you shall!"

"Yes," said the other sadly; "you have seen to
that."

"Well, then?"

"What am I to do? I am no mountain lion, Edward!"

"Fight for her, Max!" cried Granville.

"Is it my battle, or yours?" Max demanded. "I
am no fighter; I was never meant to be. I am at
the end of an old, frayed rope. Fight your own
battles, Edward."

Through the branches, I saw Granville rise and
start to leave the tree-house, and I shrank back
out of sight behind a bush. I heard his footsteps—
and only his—go past me, down the path, and die
away; all was silent. Bending aside the spiky
branches, I peered up at the tree-house, but seeing
no one, I stepped out from behind my hiding
place and went boldly up to the house itself, and
looked in the window. No one was there; the
house was empty, dusty and uncared for just as
it had been the first time I had seen it; and coiled
on the floor, a length of old rope. I waited for it
to uncoil and hiss at me, but it just lay there; and
after a while I went away.

I walked slowly down the hill, wondering
what to think and what to do. I told myself that I
had just witnessed something that had never happened, but just the same, I was shaken by it. The
illusion was too perfect; I couldn't convince my-

self that there had been no one there except Granville, for I could still hear Max's voice, unhappy and aggrieved: "Fight your own battles, Edward!" Yet, if it was illusion—why? and for whose benefit? Surely not for mine! Was it simply a trick without purpose?

My thoughts ended in the same confusion in which they began.

Unless of course—was it possible that Granville was mad? But then, I thought, who was Nina? An attendant? A nurse?

She seemed too young for such a role; but it was at least an answer, and I felt my heart grow lighter. It would explain everything, her presence in the house, even her unwillingness to talk about herself or her employers.

But it didn't explain her answer when I asked her if she, too, were living in one of Granville's stories. And it didn't explain the mountain lion.

So I was left with the puzzle as before.

What was it Granville had said? "They are not imaginary." He was speaking about the people in his books. Yet Max was a voice brought up out of a length of old rope—(or from the living coil of a snake?)—and the cougar was a shadow, half-seen, or perhaps not seen at all.

Only Nina was real, evident, and wholly present.

Was the half-world of illusion a real world to him, then? in which a rope becomes a man, and a girl walks with a mountain lion?

Dinner was unusually silent that night, for Nina appeared tired and Granville moody and preoccupied. I noticed that the Mexican woman kept his wine glass filled, and that he was drinking more than usual. Twice Nina reached over and moved his glass away from him, and each time he moved it back again with a kind of careless impatience.

All at once he struck the table with his fist. "Damn!" he said. "I hate to grow old!"

He paused, staring at us both. "Tell me," he demanded; "why do I vex myself with an old man's love affairs? Have I nothing better to do?"

Nina's expression was a curious mixture of sympathy and something else; I couldn't read it. Was it amusement? "No," she said; "you haven't."

He glared at her across the table, and she gazed steadily back at him; and a moment later I saw that secret look pass between them, that look that I had seen before. Granville burst out laughing. "You're right," he said. "Poor old Max."

He sighed then, and shook his head, despondent again. "I'm afraid the boy will get the girl after all," he said.

"Of course," said Nina simply. "I knew that all along. The young lion."

She looked over at me then; it was a very different look, appealing, a little troubled, considering . . . a woman's look, and one which I couldn't fathom. I didn't know whether Granville had noticed it or not; when I glanced his way, he was staring at his empty glass. "She would be better off with Max," he said.

"For how long?"

"I'm tired," he said. "I want Virginia."

I watched her face lose its color. "No, Edward," she said. "Please. Not yet. Not now."

"Well, then—when?"

"When you know," she said. "When you don't need me anymore."

Granville threw back his head, and sang:

> *When I came down from By-the-sea,*
> *There were two angels came with me,*
> *My youth, my girl, and I made three.*
> *When I came down from By-the-sea.*
>
> *I lost the first, the last one too;*
> *My girl alone has loved me true,*
> *My dear, my own, that comforts me*
> *When I came down from By-the-sea.*

"I'm drunk, Virginia," he said quietly, and fell out of his chair onto the floor.

I helped him to his feet, and the two of us, one on either side, got him up the stairs and into his own room. I left him there with Nina; nurse, attendant, sweetheart, friend, whatever she was, she was more able to cope with him than I was. I had a feeling that it wasn't the first time.

But it was uncomfortable for me, and I was uneasy until she came downstairs again. I kept remembering how he had spoken his wife's name:

"I'm drunk, Virginia." It seemed pitiful somehow; and it must have hurt Nina in any case.

She came back, looking drawn and weary, and the lines of her face a little blurred. She gave me her hand in a childlike way which I found very moving. "Thank you," she said.

I felt that we had been drawn together in a new intimacy. "I have to talk to you," I said; but she drew her hand away. "Yes," she said. "But not now. Not here."

"Where then? And why not now?"

"Because," she said. She looked away, and shook her head helplessly. I supposed she was thinking of Granville, sodden and asleep upstairs.

"The tree-house then?" I urged. "Tomorrow?"

I thought that she nodded her head ever so slightly. "I must go," she whispered. "Good night, Michael."

And she was gone.

I expected to lie awake for hours, thinking about her, remembering the way she looked, the way she moved, remembering the things she had said . . . but I fell asleep almost at once.

Drifting off, I was happy. I was like a young lion.

CHAPTER

9

But in the morning there was heavy fog along the coast, and when I went to the tree-house, she wasn't there. Only the coil of rope was on the floor as before.

I walked back down the hill feeling as gray and cold as the weather, and went in to see if Granville was awake; however, he was still in bed, not sleeping, but sick and irritable. "Once I could drink a whole bottle of Burgundy," he said, "but my glory has departed. Time for Nimue to clap me inside a tree, where I belong."

He smiled ruefully. "Though I find myself kicking and screaming at the very thought of it," he admitted. "I fight dissolution, Mr. Robb; I do not 'go gentle into that good night'!"

He closed his eyes. "That's Dylan Thomas," he remarked; "the only poem of his I ever understood. But then, I understand very little of today's poetry, or art, either."

I kept silent; after all, I hadn't come to Stonecliff to instruct Edward Granville in the modern idiom. Besides, he had called me Mr. Robb; apparently we were on a less friendly footing now, and I wondered how much he knew or guessed of my feeling for Nina, and wondered—again—about his own.

Mr. Granville was obviously in no mood to work on the biography, so I decided to take the morning off, and to spend it, not on the hill, but by the water. We were still in fog, but I expected it to clear as usual later on; and taking a sweater and one of Granville's early novels, I found the little rocky path to the sea, and climbed down the cliffside to the shingle.

I came down into a small, fog-shrouded cove, among dark rocks. Even a week ago I would have thought it melancholy, but now it was somehow comforting; in a curious way it seemed to fold me into the strangeness of the place, of Stonecliff and its mystery; the gray-green water rolling slowly in from nowhere, from invisible horizons, gave me a sense of other worlds and other ages of time. The fog shut out the present; damp, clinging, sea-odorous, it closed me away, and the slow surge of water lapping and hissing among the weedy stones drew me toward a timeless past.

I don't know how long I sat there in the gray air, lulled by the sound of the sea. It must have been well toward noon when I heard footsteps on the shingle, and turning, saw Nina coming toward me. She stood for a moment looking at me, then let herself down onto the pebbly sand beside me.

"Why didn't you come to the tree-house?" I asked.

"I'm sorry, Michael," she said. "I should have told you last night. I couldn't meet you there. It's Edward's place . . . Mr. Granville's. No one else goes there."

"Except Max," I said.

She gave me a startled glance. "He was there yesterday," I told her. "Mr. Granville was talking to him.

"Unless," I added, "he was talking to himself."

She was silent for a long time, hands clasped around her knees, rocking gently backwards and forwards. "He wasn't talking to himself," she said at last.

"You don't understand, do you." It was a statement, not a question.

"No," I said.

She sighed. "He does things with the heart," she said.

"You mean he's a wizard?"

"Yes."

"The last of the old Druids. And are you Nimue?" I asked lightly.

"No," she said. She stared out at the fog as though there were something out there to see. "I hope not," she said, more to herself than to me.

"Don't you know?"

76

She seemed surprised at my insistence. "It hasn't anything to do with you, Michael," she said gently.

"I'm not sure," I declared; and turned and looked at her.

She stopped rocking, and sat very still, her chin on her knees, staring back at me. After a while she said, "Michael—don't."

"Why not, Nina?"

She shook her head, still looking up at me from under her dark lashes. "If you mean what I think you mean . . ." she said.

I picked up a stone, and threw it toward the sea. "Is he in love with you?" I asked.

Her voice trembled ever so slightly when she replied, "He is in love with his wife;" and she looked at me bravely.

I tried not to sound as heavy hearted as I felt. "Tell me about her," I urged. "What is she like— Mrs. Granville—Virginia?"

"I can't," she said. "Don't ask me, Michael."

A pelican came floating in from the foggy sea, skimming along the air above the waves, and came to rest just outside the surf-line. He rode the swells, preening the feathers on his breast and neck, and gazing at us solemnly. I threw a stone at him, and with a guttural cry he rose heavily with slowly beating wings and planed off into the fog again.

"He has to be in love in order to write," I remarked, looking at Nina sideways. "He told me so himself."

"I know," she said.

I wanted desperately to cry out to her, "Are you in love with him?" but I didn't dare. What if she said "Yes?" It was better not to know . . .

"Nina," I asked, half seriously, "are you under some kind of spell?"

I expected her to laugh at me. Instead, she stretched her hand out toward me for a moment, and then drew it back again and folded it with the other in her lap. "We both are, Michael," she said gravely. "Didn't you know?"

I threw myself back onto the shingle, and stared up at the unseen sky. I felt helpless and weary; where was I? In what strange country of the heart? *We both are* . . . Did she feel it too?

"Do you care for me at all?" I asked, and held my breath.

She was a long time answering. "Yes," she said at last, in a small voice.

I took it to mean more than it did, and drew in a deep sigh of air. "I think I'm in love with you," I declared.

Her answer was colder on my heart than the fog. "You mustn't be," she said. "I mustn't let you." And, more gently,

"It's impossible."

"Why impossible?"

She didn't answer. We sat stiff and silent, staring straight ahead, and the fog blew in on us, damp and cold. I tried to smile. "I suppose the pelican was another of his characters," I said. "Or was it Granville himself?"

"Perhaps," she replied indifferently. I gave a little laugh, but my heart was heavy. "Well, after all," I said, "why not? Max is a coil of old rope. And there's the cougar . . ."

I must have spoken more bitterly than I'd meant to, because I knew at once that I'd made her unhappy. "Oh, Michael!" she whispered; "Must you?"

I wasn't very pleased with myself. "I'm sorry," I said; "Forget it."

She sighed, and looked at me, and then away, out to the fog-shrouded sea. "You make it very difficult," she said.

I felt a sudden surge of impatience; I didn't want to be put off like a child, gently, evasively.

"Is that all I mean to you?" I demanded. "Is that what you want me to believe?"

"Yes," she said steadily. "I want you to believe that."

"It isn't true," I said. "And I don't believe it."

"Oh," she cried in distress, "the truth . . . who knows what the truth is?"

"The truth is that I love you."

She got to her feet deliberately and brushed the sand from her legs. "It's time for lunch," she said. "Edward will be waiting."

We climbed back up the cliff together, Nina a step ahead of me and above me. I wanted to reach out to her—but I knew that I could never win her against her will. And there was another thought, a sobering one: that we might very likely tumble, the both of us, ingloriously down the cliff to the bottom.

Granville was in the living room waiting for us when we came in. Nina swept upstairs without a word, and Granville turned to me with a curious expression.

"The ocean is very cold at this time of year," he said.

His voice seemed hoarse; I thought, for a moment, that he sounded like a pelican.

CHAPTER

10

For the rest of the day we went on with the work, but Granville seemed absent-minded, and inclined to wander off onto other subjects. At one point he picked up a small stone carving from his desk, and studied it with an air of abstraction. It was a female figure, curiously attractive in the tender tilt of the head and in the rounded, womanly shoulders, but with an enormous belly, and buttocks like huge melons. He told me that it was a copy of the famous Venus of Lespugue from distant Paleolithic times, and that it probably represented the Earth Goddess. "We can only guess, of course," he said; "for it is not known in what esteem our earliest ancestors held their wives.

"To both the Greeks and the Romans, the Goddess of Wisdom was a woman. What is surprising is that, although wisdom was highly esteemed in those days, women were not. That the

Goddess of Love was also a woman is not as surprising, for in the mythologies she is usually pictured as being not very bright."

I wondered why he had chosen to talk about love, and in such a way—although I was inclined to agree with him that the Goddess of Love was not very bright.

"Of course," I said, trying to sound intelligent, "in the past the education of women . . ."

Granville went on as though I hadn't said anything. "Possibly," he remarked, "in seeking to change this state of affairs, we have helped to dig our own graves. After all, it was Merlin who taught the nymph Nimue the spell by which she was later able to undo him. He was obliged to do so, for he couldn't abide a stupid woman, although she attracted him. He was in love with wisdom; when he had taught Nimue all he knew, he found her irresistible, and she clapped him into a tree."

"I'm not sure I understand you," I said. "In your books you speak very differently about love." And I quoted from his best-known novel: "*I only know that we were meant to be together, that the strands of her life were woven in with mine; and that even time and the world could not part us altogether. Not then. Not ever.*'

"I thought that was what you believed," I said.

He smiled, a little sadly. "I did not mean," he said, "that love would outlast the elements. But it is very strong; once rooted, like the ivy it persists. I myself . . ."

He stopped, and considered; he seemed to draw back into himself, into memories. "Long before I met Virginia," he said at last, "in fact, while she was still a child, I met and loved a woman older than myself. If a man can be said to have one great love in his youth, she was that love. She was gentle, tender, and patient; she dared everything in the world for me except marriage; for one thing, she was already married. Our affair lasted for ten years—years of almost unbearable anguish and unbelievable raptures. In the end, we parted, not without sorrow."

"How could you have left each other," I asked, wondering "if you were so in love?"

He shook his head uncertainly. "Somewhere in those ten years," he said, "we lost each other. You ask me if love is eternal, if it never dies; and I tell you that as long as it is remembered, it lives on. My mistress lives on in my memory just as she was in the past, young, tender, and breathtakingly beautiful. And I live there with her—young too, and not at all wise."

I found myself, to my surprise, very much touched by the old man's story, and once again envious of the fullness of his life. Would I ever be able to speak so lovingly of anyone? To remember beauty and wonder . . . ? Would I ever have such a love to remember? the pain worn away by the years, and only the shining left . . . ? Despite myself, I felt myself drawn to him, mystery and all.

He gave me a gentle smile. "It will last as long

as I do," he said. "As long as there is anyone left to remember it."

"And after?"

He raised his hands in a puzzled gesture. "Logic rejects it," he said. "But certainly, in an incomprehensible universe, nothing is impossible."

He seemed embarrassed, as though he had said more than he'd meant to; and soon afterwards he dismissed me, and retired for his customary nap. He didn't come down for dinner, but had a tray brought up to him; Nina was absent, too, and I was left alone at table with my thoughts. I kept remembering how she had said, "You make it very difficult." Yet, I thought, there had been regret in her voice. "I mustn't let you," she had said. Did that mean that she was not altogether indifferent—despite everything?

I went to bed early, with my heart full of conflicting hopes and doubts, near-avowals, and contradictions. This is insane, I thought, it's no good for me; I should leave this place at once . . . tomorrow . . . before it's too late . . .

The last thing I remember hearing was an owl hooting somewhere far away. "I've heard that bird before," I said, and slept.

I woke . . . or did I wake? . . . some time before dawn. It was still dark; but looking toward the window, I thought I could make out the faint illumination cast by the lamp in Granville's study onto the hillside below. Was he still at work, drawing his world like a web around him? All was silent, except for the sound of the sea, which seemed a little louder than usual. I drew my sweater on over my pyjamas, and opening my door, tiptoed into the hall and down the stairs.

Granville was at his desk, his head bent over his work, his pencil patiently crawling across the sheet of paper in front of him. He seemed to be unaware of my presence; I stood there (if indeed I was there at all), while the room, the house, and Granville himself slowly disappeared, seeming to draw away from me into the darkness, leaving me behind in another night and in another place.

I was no longer in a room; I was on a wide beach, where fires in fire-rings burned yellow and bright in the blue, sea-evening air. Around me, up and down the beach, families were bent over their cooking; children were playing, and couples wandered in and out of shadow and fire-light, or lay together near the flames, screened by a blanket against the night-wind from the sea. Behind them the ocean rose and fell, tumbling in hollow thunder on the shore.

I had no sense of being asleep, or in a dream; I was awake, or so it seemed to me. All the sounds were muted, but clear, as though heard not so much by the outer as by the inner ear. I felt the cold night-air. I smelled the sea. I felt the sand under my feet. I observed it all without surprise. I was there—and not there.

I watched a boy and a girl rise from beside one of the fires, and start up the beach together; and I went with them. The yellow firelight dwindled away behind them, leaving small circles of gold in the sand. A star blazed for a moment across the sky, falling in a long arc, and the girl said "Make a wish."

She turned and held out her hand to the boy, and he caught up with her and took her hand for a moment and then let it go. They went on together side by side, their feet half in the water as it ran up the beach, and half in wet sand.

Was the girl Nina? I couldn't tell: they were only two young, shadowy figures. It was too dark —or else I was too far away—to see their faces. The girl was slender, like Nina. The boy moved with the strong, clumsy grace of a young lion.

Where the beach curved inward a little way, she turned back from the water and walked by herself up the sloping sand into the deeper darkness of the bluff, and began to slip out of her dress. "I'm going in," she called back to the boy. I could see the white glimmer of her body as she let her dress fall; it was all shadowy and indistinct. A moment later she was running down the sand, with that curious, light, flying, awkward movement of a young girl, and had flung herself under a wave.

The boy undressed slowly, and went hesitatingly down to the sea, and into the water gingerly. The water was dark, and I knew that he was lonely and afraid. "Halys," he called across the water; "Halys!"

She came in then, over a rising comber, her hair floating out behind her. "I thought I'd lost you," he cried out, and "Did you?" she called back from the crest of the wave.

Unaccountably, I felt a flood of happiness, a profound relief; some tension in me suddenly gave way, and I seemed to draw back into myself from somewhere far away, from something troubling and strange . . . The distant fire-rings down the beach began to burn more dimly; the sound of the surf dwindled to a low, far-off murmur; and the boy and the girl and the beach itself seemed to dissolve into a shimmer of soft light . . .

And then I was back at Stonecliff again, in the hall outside Granville's study. He had laid down his pencil, and was sitting quietly staring straight ahead at nothing in front of him. I thought that he looked tired, and sad.

I turned, and made my way quietly up the stairs to my own room. I don't remember getting back into bed; perhaps—for all I know—I had never left it. Yet I had a feeling that I had seen something I wasn't supposed to see, been somewhere I was never meant to be . . . I was uncertain of everything; I only knew that the great owl on his silent, dark wings, was still calling from far away above the hills.

I awoke with a sense of urgency, with the conviction that there was something I had to find out, something I had to know. Was I in love with a girl in a story? . . . someone made out of (how had he put it?) fog and rain and flowering bushes . . . and love (*his* love?) and memory . . . ?

The boy on that dream-like beach had called the girl Halys. It was a strange name, but I thought that I had heard it before, though I didn't remember where. Anyway, it wasn't Nina; and that was the important thing.

Still—I had to know. Had I been dreaming? I must have been. But was I dreaming asleep? . . . or awake?

There was no one about after breakfast when I went into Granville's study, but on his desk was the page of manuscript from the night before. I went over and stared down at it.

And there in Granville's pencilled scrawl, just as I had heard it, was the name:

"Halys."

And *"She came in then over a rising comber . . ."*

CHAPTER

11

So whatever Nina was, she wasn't the girl in
Granville's new novel. Halys was an illusion, a
creature born in the dark hours of the night by
someone working late and lonely . . . doing
things with the heart.

If only Granville's wife would return! I felt
that her absence was itself part of the mystery,
and that her presence alone would solve it. But I
remembered, too, that when I had suggested waiting for her, Granville had discouraged me. Why?
Could there be some trouble between Granville
and his wife? Yet Nina had been quite certain that
he loved her, and Granville had as much as admitted it himself.

What then? What reason could there be—except the fact of Nina's presence in the house? I
didn't want to believe it, and yet no other reason
presented itself. On the other hand, Nina had

spoken of Mrs. Granville as though she knew her; almost, in fact, as though they were friends. Surely, then, her place in the household could be no secret to Granville's wife.

No; nothing that I had heard suggested any trouble between the two women. On the contrary, it seemed to me that Nina accepted Granville's love for Virginia as though, in some way, it was a comfort to her.

It was Granville, after all, who confused me. Was he really the amiable, scholarly gentleman he seemed—or was there something darker about him, some shadow of a warlock? I no longer thought that he had been speaking idly when he told me that he created his own world, for I had seen it myself. Or had I? I found it impossible to make up my mind. Perhaps I should have been afraid of him, but I wasn't; on the contrary, I felt drawn to him in some kind of sympathy, or perhaps pity. How long could he hope to hold so young a girl as Nina in this sea-and-mountain solitude? For no matter what reason; with no matter what spells.

I found him sitting on the terrace, gazing moodily out to sea. "Ah," he said; "Mr. Robb. Did you have a quiet night?"

"I had a curious dream," I said. "I was on a fire-beach somewhere in the south . . ."

He nodded indifferently. "Yes," he said without surprise; "I thought you were there. Did it seem familiar to you?"

I stared at him warily. "Should it have?" I asked.

"It is a beach not far from where you live," he said. "And the boy . . . ? Did you think you knew the boy?"

"No," I said. "I didn't know him."

He thought that over for a moment or two; it seemed to puzzle him. "Are you sure?" he asked at last. "After all—I haven't met *many* young men lately."

I remembered then suddenly, how I had known how the boy felt, afraid of the loneliness and the darkness of the sea. "But the girl's name was Halys," I said, watching him.

He looked at me uncertainly. "Yes," he said. "Why not?"

"It wasn't anyone I knew," I said, "and I was afraid it would be."

He gave me a curiously startled look, and then I saw his face grow blank, his expression turn inward. He seemed to be making up his mind to something, slowly, brooding above the ocean like a cormorant on its rock. Finally, "Do you know the story of King David," he asked, "in his later years?"

"Do you mean Abishag the Shunamite?"

"She lay in David's bosom," he said. "To warm him when he was old."

I, too, remembered my Bible. "But he knew her not!" I exclaimed impulsively.

Granville regarded me coldly. "She was only there to warm him," he said.

I thought that he was telling me that all he wanted of Nina was her youth, her young presence; and I felt a rush of gratitude and relief. But at the same time, some inner sense held me back—warned me against him, told me that it wasn't as simple as that, that it couldn't be. Because he must resent me—my youth, my presence there—just as in my own way I resented his position, his experience . . . and whatever it was of Nina that he had taken for himself.

And yet, I felt a need to comfort him; perhaps because, for all his wisdom, he seemed so vulnerable. "After all," I told him, "David was at the end of his life."

He nodded somberly. "Yes," he said; "and I suppose you mean that I am not. That is kind of you; and I thank you for it. But when David died, an age died with him—the age of greatness in Israel. Already, in Solomon's time, the fruit had started to decay of too much sweet. And what my own spirit craves warmth against is not my own, singular dissolution—though I admit, I cannot relish its approach—but the ending of an age, the age of the humanities. It is dying of its own poison—a curious forbearance, almost an inertia, a paralysis of will."

" *'But like the serpent that with poisoned breath,'* " I reminded him, " *'Bites its own wound and stings itself to death.'* "

"I wish you'd stop quoting me!" said Granville fretfully. "Besides, it's the adder, not the serpent."

He shook his head, frowning at the interruption to his thoughts. "The age of forbearance," he said. "It brings about its own downfall. It stretches its neck beneath the guillotine with no more than a regretful sigh."

All at once he broke off, and rising to his feet with an exclamation, gestured vigorously in the direction of the driveway which approached the house from below. Following his gaze, I saw Nina emerge from the trees, at the same time that a grocer's delivery wagon from Los Olivos started up the short road to the house.

There was no danger, as far as I could see, no need for alarm; there was plenty of room in the driveway, and in any case, all Nina had to do was stand to one side until the wagon had passed. Instead, to my surprise, she shrank back among the trees as though she were afraid of being seen or recognized, and—as far as I could tell—disappeared from sight altogether.

Granville resumed his seat as though nothing had happened; and the delivery wagon having stopped at the house, he asked the driver to take the groceries around to the kitchen in back. The driver, a pleasant young man, did so, and afterwards stopped to exchange a few remarks about the weather which he felt was fixing to turn bad. "And how is Mrs. Granville?" he asked; to which Granville replied that his wife was in good health, but still away.

An ordinary moment of an ordinary day, I would have said—except that it wasn't ordinary at all. It was plain that the grocer's man knew

Granville's wife, Virginia—and that he didn't know Nina. Or perhaps he did; but in any case, it was equally plain that Granville didn't want him to see her. It made me sad; I felt sorry for Granville, and for Nina, and although I didn't like to admit it, I felt sorry for myself too.

For the rest of the day and the evening, I was left with the feeling of perplexity with which I had been living ever since my arrival at Stonecliff —and with a bad taste in my mouth, besides. For now I was disappointed in Granville; I hated to have him seem so ordinary—an old man with his wife away and his Shunamite hidden in the woods. He was too distinguished a writer for that.

A sharp wind came in that night, blowing down from a ridge of high pressure in the north. It was clear and cold, and made the stars glitter; I went to sleep hearing the wind moving in the hills. I woke to the sound of my door being opened; I thought it had been blown open by the wind, but it was shut again, gently.

I raised myself on one elbow and peered through the darkness. I held my breath in the stillness, listening, and a tiny ripple of chill played up and down my arms. There was no sound; but I could feel that someone was in the room with me.

For a moment I had the wild hope that it might be Nina. But as my eyes grew accustomed to the dark, I made out a darker silhouette seated against the faint star-shine of the window; and it wasn't Nina. I felt a sudden, irrational moment of fear—

of the unknown, rather than of anything actual
—and in the silence I felt my breath catch in my
throat.

"You're awake," said Granville's voice out of
the blackness.

At once—and again, for no reason—I felt a
flood of relief. "Yes," I said. "What is it?"

He didn't answer at once. There seemed to be
a greater darkness in the corner where he was, as
though he had drawn into himself all the shadows
of the night. When he spoke at last, it was in little more than a whisper; I wasn't even sure that
I had heard him.

"I am hag-ridden," he said.

After a while he continued in a mournful voice,
"Why do you persist?"

I couldn't tell whether he was talking to me,
or to someone beyond me, some shadowy figure
in his mind.

"I am being led in the wrong direction," he
said. "It is not the direction in which I want to
go."

His words sounded slurred, and I wondered if
he had been drinking again. "Mr. Granville," I
said, "let me help you to your room."

"No!" he said sharply; and then, clearly,

"I need no help from you, Jon!"

Jon? . . . But who was Jon? from what unknown pages of Granville's life? I wondered if I
ought not try to find Nina; she would know, better than I, what to do, how to deal with this situation. Perhaps between the two of us . . .

But he seemed to guess my thoughts. "No one can help me," he declared. "Once the spell is begun, it goes on to the end. And we go deeper with it . . . deeper and deeper . . ."

He stirred in his chair by the window, and I could feel him looking at me. "I have been to the fire-beach again," he said. "I thought . . . I thought . . ."

His voice trailed away. "No one would listen to me," he said. "No one would believe . . ."

He gave a deep sigh. "I'm old," he said and got to his feet. His shadow filled all one end of the room. "My powers are in eclipse," he said.

He was moving slowly toward the door. "At some point . . ." he seemed to be fumbling with his thoughts . . . "at some point . . . have I lost the sense of being right?"

His fingers found the knob, and he went out, closing the door gently behind him. The wind had died; it was no longer moving in the hills. The house was full of silence.

Once again I vowed to leave the next morning. But I fell asleep almost immediately, and slept peacefully through the night.

CHAPTER

———

12

I forgot about leaving Stonecliff; I woke up thinking of Nina. But she was not there when I came downstairs.

Instead, I found Granville in his study, doing his setting-up exercises. He looked old, untidy, wrinkled and creased with sleep; I was embarrassed for him, and started to leave, but he motioned me to stay. "In the morning," he said, "my joints are stiff, but my spirits are good; I have lived through another night, and have a whole new day ahead of me. Anything could happen; the day is full of hope . . . for a while, anyway; it is only my body that drags a little."

I wondered if he remembered having visited me during the night and whether I should mention it. "Do you feel all right, sir?" I asked. "Last night it seemed to me . . ."

"At night," Granville went on as though I

hadn't spoken, "it is exactly the opposite. All I can think of is death."

Yes, I thought: that's the wrong direction for anyone. But I didn't say anything.

"I think about it a great deal," he continued solemnly. "But when I am working at my writing it never enters my mind, because then I am living, and to the living, death isn't something to worry about. That is why God cannot be dead, as people claim; because to create is to be alive."

I remarked that he had written a great deal about death.

" 'Who nothing sees, sees nothing to dismay;
Who nothing knows, knows not what nothing is,' "

He made a grimace. "That's just it," he said: "that 'nothing.' I lie in the dark and try to imagine what being nothing must be like—but I can't. The human mind clings to its sense of something. Even in sleep."

He let himself down heavily behind his desk. "I often wonder what it must be like to be an insect," he said, "and to be unaware of death as a condition; to think of it merely as an event, as the moth must think of it (if he thinks at all) at the moment he is flattened by a blow. That must have been the state of Adam and Eve in the Garden, before they ate the fruit of the Tree of Knowledge . . . a joyous, springtime innocence; two ignorant creatures, unmindful of the past or the future. When they broke God's command, and became people, they learned—among other things—that they would have to die. That was the curse God put upon them.

"It must have been like a thunder-clap in the world: the end of Eternity, and the beginning of Time. All creatures suddenly knew themselves for what they were: the lion as well as the lamb, the spider, the lizard, and the fly . . . And all began to act according to their natures.

"What a commotion! What a sudden bleating and buzzing, roaring and squealing!"

"It's an amusing idea," I said, "though I wouldn't call it biologically sound."

"Of course it isn't," he agreed; "it's pure Fundamentalism."

He stopped, and regarded me darkly. "How old are you, Mr. Robb?" he asked.

"I'm thirty-two, sir," I said.

He seemed surprised. "I would have thought you younger," he declared. "At thirty-two, I had already conquered the world. I was Shelley, Voltaire, Cervantes; I was Augustus, Alexander . . . David . . ."

Turning away with a sudden gesture of impatience, he banged his fist on his desk. "Ak!" he cried; "what is the good of all that now? I'm not David, I'm Saul; and if I had a javelin, I'd hurl it at you!"

I stared at him in astonishment, thinking that I'd like to hurl something at him myself. And then he swung around again and smiled at me disarmingly. "I'm in a bad mood," he said; "forgive me."

I nodded briefly. "I think I'll spend the rest of the day working over my notes," I said. "If you don't mind."

"Do," he agreed. "By all means. And if you see Nina . . ."

He paused uncertainly. "No need to say anything about last night," he said, and turned back to his desk again.

It was the only mention he made of having visited me.

I worked all day in my room, trying to bring some order to my notes—trying to find, in the tangle of illusion and bewilderment, some strand of reality. Had I been dreaming at times—asleep? —awake? And Nina? How could I describe her, how explain her? I could find no key.

And always, in the end, I came back to Virginia Granville; the harder I tried to find a center, a focus for my thoughts, the more I came to realize that the focal point had to be in Granville's wife. She alone held the clue to Granville's life and character; she alone could define Nina; only she could tell me how much of the mystery I was living in, awake or asleep, was Merlin, and how much was moonshine.

And the more I worked, the angrier I grew. Or perhaps not so much angry, as resentful—because I didn't know what I was angry at. There was something between Nina and Granville that I didn't understand; there was something between

Nina and myself, which kept us apart, and which she wouldn't explain.

It was like trying to find my way to a strange place in a fog. And actually, in the late afternoon, the fog started to come in from the sea; and soon after that it was dark.

It must have been nearly eight o'clock when there was a knock on my door, and when I opened it, there was Nina. She had on her sweater, and her hair was damp; she must have just come in from outside. "Michael," she said; "Where is Edward?"

"I've no idea," I said blankly. "In his study, I suppose—isn't he?"

"No," she said, "he isn't. He's not anywhere."

"Well," I said, rubbing my eyes, "I imagine he'll turn up when he's ready."

But she was concerned; she wanted to know when I'd seen him last. When I told her that I hadn't seen him all day, she seemed worried. I told her that he'd been comparing himself to Saul. "Oh," she said bleakly; "that's a bad mood."

"I was the one he threw the javelin at," I said.

"We've got to find him," she said. She gave me a blurry look. "Did he hurt you?" she asked.

"It wasn't a real javelin," I said, "I'm sure he's all right. He may have driven to Los Olivos."

"I'd have heard the car," she said. "Or you would have. Anyway—he doesn't like to drive. And in this fog—"

She looked around her with a worried, helpless expression. "I'm going out to look for him," she said. "You don't have to come if you don't want to."

"Don't be silly," I said. "Of course I want to."

And, strangely enough, I did. I didn't want to care about Granville—but I did.

I wondered why she was so worried. "What could have happened to him?" I asked.

"He could have fallen," she said. "He could be lost. The cliff . . ."

"Yes," I said. "Let's go."

She had a flashlight; she put a shawl around her shoulders, and a raincoat over that, and I had a heavy sweater, but the fog reached into us as soon as we went outside. It was like going into cold water, and not being able to see more than a few feet in any direction. The beam of Nina's torch made a little glow in front of us, but it was a diffused light; it showed us the ground at our feet and not much more. We went in Indian-file, with Nina ahead, and every now and then she would call out "Edward!"—and we would stop and listen.

It was hard to know where we were; and almost at once the whole search struck me as hopeless. And not only hopeless, but frightening; I felt that we were as lost as Granville. Yet Nina seemed to know her way; she led me surely through the woods and down the rocky path to the shore. I wondered if she thought Granville had gone into the water.

"Edward," she called; and called again. I could hear the worry in her voice.

"Edward! Where are you?" But there was no reply.

It was even colder down there by the water, and I had a hard time keeping my teeth from chattering. "Has he ever done this before?" I asked.

She threw the beam of her torch against the water, but all it showed us was the fog, peach-colored where the light hit it. "Yes," she said.

"And you had to find him?"

She hesitated a moment before replying. "Somebody had to," she said at last, and clicked off her light, and moved away.

At once the darkness and the loneliness of the night rushed over me. "Nina!" I cried, "Nina!"

Her light flicked on again, a few feet away. "Did you think you'd lost me too?" she asked.

And suddenly I was back at the fire-beach in the moonlight, with the girl Halys. It was a strange sensation, and it only lasted a moment, and then the fog closed in again, and I was where I was. But the fear, the sense of panic, was gone. I had a feeling that it had all been arranged, that everything was the way it had to be, and that it would turn out all right in the end.

"We'll try the tree-house," she said.

She passed me, and I turned to follow; our feet made wet sounds on the shingle. The separate footsteps overlapped, and seemed to draw us together in a single sound. We climbed the slippery, stony path again, Nina in front, the light of her torch floating like a great yellow moth over the half-seen rocks and bushes, and everything beyond its beam lost in the darkness.

I could sense that Nina's mood had changed, some dread had lifted from her spirit. Granville was not down there among the stones. Her feet seemed lighter on the path; and mine were, too.

She didn't call out his name any more. Among the trees, we spoke in whispers; we were like hunters, like children playing at hide-and-seek in the dark. The fog made a circle of secrecy around us, a hiding place of silence; and our breaths, puffs of mist in the icy air, lost themselves in the greater mist enfolding us. I felt light-hearted; my whole life seemed to tremble on the brink of some unimaginable happiness. "Nina," I whispered.

She placed her hand for a moment over mine; I was surprised at how soft and cold it was. "Hush," she said, and we stopped and stood still, holding our breaths and listening. I could hear my heart beating; and then a sound somewhere in the night ahead of us, a murmur, very faint, little more than a vibration in the air . . . a voice, perhaps? or voices? "What is it?" I asked, my lips close to her ear. I could smell the faint fragrance of her hair.

She turned her face toward me. "It's the tree-house," she whispered. "There's someone there."

CHAPTER

13

We went forward slowly, hand in hand, feeling our way among the trees, and reached the top of the slope above the tree-house, and saw below us the faint, diffused glow of a lantern. "Edward," Nina called; but I noticed that she called softly, and clicked off her torch, leaving us in the dark.

We stood looking down, and listening. We couldn't see the house itself, only the yellow, faint light in the fog; but we could hear the voices. There were two of them: I heard Granville, and then another man. I knew that voice; I had heard it before. "It's Max," I whispered, and Nina nodded her head. "I know," she whispered back.

Max was talking. "It's no good, Edward," I heard him say; "it is all useless. No matter how you try: The girl is not in love with me. You cannot change nature."

"I know that," said Granville heavily. "Still— love comes and goes."

"For some," said Max wryly, "but not for me. I do not fool myself; love doesn't come to me, at my age. I don't even dream any longer."

"I'm sorry, Max," said Granville.

"I am lonely," Max admitted, "but not as unhappy as I might be, considering. Actually, I think I would enjoy being alone for a while; I would value it. Allow me that luxury, Edward."

"I cannot," said Granville coldly. "You forget: we have a book to write."

"I know," said Max bitterly; "a love-story. A war, a duel between myself and youth. And how does it come out? It is even stupid of me to ask. Just fancy: I take a young girl off the beach, to live with me. Is that a dream for a young girl— to live with an old man? And for me—what kind of a life is that? I even allow myself to imagine . . ."

"*I* allow you to," Granville corrected him.

"To what good? Probably she will leave me for a younger man. It happens every day to somebody; tomorrow it can happen to me. This battle I do not want; I can lose it. So much anguish for nothing!"

She hasn't left you yet," said Granville. "What's more, she loves you, in her way . . . or I think she does. Nothing is decided yet."

"There are grades of love," said Max, "like eggs and butter. What an old man feels for a young woman, and what a young woman feels

106

for a young man, are not the same thing at all. Those rockets in the blood, those pinwheels and Roman candles that I remember from my youth, make no uproar in her breast . . . nor, to be quite honest, in mine. I no longer feel that exaltation of the senses, which, combined with jealousy and a nervous stomach, once told me that I was young and happy."

"It's a mistake," said Granville wearily, "to think of youth as a time of happiness. It's an intense time, and ankle deep in suffering. All the answers for which a young man waits are still ahead of him."

There was silence for a moment. "And the answers for which an old man waits?" asked Max softly; "where are they?"

"Ah," said Granville slowly; "where indeed? I shall be very frightened when I come to die."

"What!" exclaimed Max. "I thought the answer was love!

"I am only repeating what is in your books," he added.

"I was younger then," said Granville. "I was an eagle in love. Now I am old, pushed from the nest, watching the young eaglets fighting to see who shall inherit . . ."

"Very fancy," said Max. "Actually, you are an old goose, pushed with all the other old geese out of the pond. So now, perhaps, the answer isn't love?"

"Sometimes," said Granville, "lying alone at night, I have my doubts."

"Then find me another answer," said Max.

In the silence which followed, I thought I heard Nina crying, very softly. I put my hand to her cheek, and it came away wet. She shook her head angrily, but whether at herself or at me, I couldn't tell.

Granville said nothing for a long while. Then, "I'm afraid you will have to find it for yourself, Max," he said at last.

I heard Nina give a long, shuddering sigh, and I turned toward her—whether to question or to comfort, I wasn't sure—and caught a sudden glimpse over her shoulder of a vague shape that, even as I gazed, vanished dim and fog-like among the trees. It was only a glimpse; and I could have been mistaken. But it looked, in the fraction of a second that I saw it, like the shape of a great cat, a cougar or a mountain lion. It could have been part of the fog itself, it was so silent and incorporeal.

Granville was speaking again.

"There is no answer, old friend," he said. "There is no way to escape the loneliness of life."

"I am not your friend," said Max.

It was the end of the conversation. I heard Granville get to his feet, and the creak of boards as he left the tree-house. His lantern bobbed slowly off among the trees, the misty yellow glow growing fainter and fainter in the distance, until at last it was gone altogether, and we were left alone in the darkness and silence.

I had my arm around Nina, and I could feel her trembling a little, perhaps from the cold. For a moment she seemed to gather herself as though to follow him, and then she turned quiet again, and stood there dejected and uncertain. "Merlin is gone," I said. I took the torch from her hand, and clicked it on; the tree-house looked dim and dark and deserted. "Max is gone, too," I said.

She made a small, dreary sound. "It's time we went, then," she said, but she didn't move. I began to urge her gently toward the empty tree-house. "No, Michael," she said.

There was a dry rustling at our feet, and she gave a gasp and turned and clung to me, her head hidden against my shoulder. I looked down, but I couldn't see anything in the darkness. "It's nothing," I said. I bent over, and swung her off her feet, and lifted her up, and held her. Her hair was against my cheek; it was soft and light and it felt cold on my face.

I knew it had been the snake going by our feet, and I didn't want to tell her. But she must have guessed, because she didn't ask me to put her down.

I didn't know what to do. I didn't want to take her to the tree-house—not any longer; and I couldn't take her back to Stonecliff, either—not yet, not until we had faced each other honestly, and—for once—had said what we had to say. If she was in love with Granville, I wanted her to tell me so. And if not . . .

I took a step or two with her in my arms. "No, Michael," she said. "Let me go." I didn't know what else to do, so I kissed her.

For a moment I swear she kissed me back. Then she struggled free, and turned to face me. When she spoke, it was in a voice I had never heard before.

"I am not Nimue," she said.

CHAPTER

14

"Nimue? I never thought you were," I said.

It wasn't true; for I had thought her Nimue—and Abishag, and a registered nurse, and somebody made out of moonlight and sea-foam. I didn't know who she was, and I didn't care. "I love you," I said.

But again she answered as before: "No."

"Nina . . ." I began.

"Please," she begged; and put her hand against my mouth. "Don't say it, Michael. It's all wrong . . ."

I took her hand in both of mine. "I have to," I said. "You love me, too!"

"No," she whispered despairingly.

"And I say, Yes." I drew her toward me in silence. "You heard him, Nina," I told her: " 'There is no way to escape the loneliness of being alive' . . . except this!"

I had her in my arms, and I was kissing her—aware only of her fragrance, of the cold, sweet face pressed against mine, of searching, shadowy eyes, of moving lips, warm, wonderfully soft . . .

And then, suddenly, she was crying. And as I held her, perplexed and uncertain, not knowing what to do, I heard her voice, a thin, lost sound in the night—

"It's too much—too much . . . Edward—if you love me, let me go . . . release me from this spell . . ."

—and in that forlorn weeping, Granville's voice from somewhere far away,

"Not yet." It sounded weary, and infinitely sad.

The weeping passed, like a summer storm, and she was still, in a breath-held silence. "He will have to let you go," I said. "He cannot keep you. Not now. Not any more."

"Hush!" she said, and turned closer toward me. "Oh Michael," she whispered, "what am I to do?"

I felt her lips on mine, trembling, wondering, still uncertain. And then she gave herself to me in a sudden rush, wholly, with all her heart. "Yes," she whispered, "yes!"

But in the very act of embracing me, a dreadful change seemed to come over her. It was as though an icy wind had touched her. She drew away from me, and stood staring out beyond me, the long honey-dark hair tossed back from her face, her hands on her hips. "This is your fault,

Edward," she said bitterly. "I am not to be blamed."

I gaped at her in bewilderment. She stood there as though she were listening, tense and rigid. "Madness," she said bleakly. "Madness." Her voice was harsh and cold, unfamiliar—a stranger's voice, someone I had never met . . . Whoever she was, she wasn't Nina; she wasn't the girl who had sat with me at the sea's rim, had stood with me before the tree-house . . . had cooked me my breakfast that first morning . . .

I thought of Granville's nymph—deadlier than the adult; the nymph of the dragonfly . . .

"Listen!" she called defiantly into the darkness; "I'm young. That's what you wanted, isn't it?"

And a moment later, with a sound like a sob, she threw herself into my arms again, held me close, lifted her mouth to mine. "I am what you want me to be," she said in a dying voice.

Was she talking to me—or to herself—or to Granville? I thought I heard his voice again, from far away; I thought I heard him say, "I still need you," but I couldn't be sure.

And it no longer mattered to me who she was, or what she was—or to whom she was talking. Nymph, mortal, illusion, or reality, it was all one, all gathered together in an overwhelming assault upon me. All I knew was the passion which ran through my blood like music, a great chorus of longing and anguish, of triumph and joy. I had one moment of clarity, and thought, "A wizard does things with the heart" . . . but it was swept away in the storm. This was no virgin I held in my arms, no cool young girl, no untried maiden, but an ardent woman, her willing body as warm with desire as mine, her movements swift and expert, urgent, greedy . . . all in a rage of haste, as though she couldn't wait.

And all the while, behind her murmuring sighs, under her hands, between her kisses, I felt an undercurrent of loss and grief . . . something almost like despair.

The fog was around us, enfolding us, pressing us together. In the darkness, we were alone, drowning in our senses, enchanted, drawn down in a bottomless sea. "Nina," I whispered; "Nina." I repeated her name over and over, as though to hold her with it. She didn't seem to hear; she, too, was lost—as lost as I was.

I don't know how long we stood there, locked in each other's arms. I came up slowly out of a dream, only dimly aware of where I was, seeing the night around me, the cold, the fog . . . aware, too, of a commotion, itself dim and dreamlike, somewhere nearby. She must have heard it too . . . for she drew away from me, and we turned, peering into the darkness around us, shivering, trembling, our arms little by little loosing their hold, letting go of each other. There was shadowy movement near us, swift and violent, silent, intense; but we saw nothing. I bent and groped on the ground for Nina's flashlight, found it, and switched it on.

What we saw in the dim orange glow was the great tawny shape of the cougar rearing and prancing, darting and striking at something on the ground, something which struck back at him in desperation. In and out of shadow, lost in the fog, in the darkness, picked out again in the light of the torch, the great beast pounced and struck, and the long, sinewy coils whipped in and out, all in silence and terror. "Is it the snake?" I whispered; and she nodded her head. "Yes," she said, and trembled.

How long the battle raged, it is impossible to say. There were glimpses of the coiled, lashing serpent, the prancing lion; once the snake succeeded in throwing two coils around the cougar's body . . . and I felt, to my horror, a burn of pain along my ribs. Once I saw the cougar's jaws clamped on the snake's head, and watched in pity and fright as the mottled serpent writhed and twisted in agony.

Were they creatures?—or were they spirits, locked in battle? They made no sound; there was only the thrashing of branches, the rush of shadows, the fanning of the air. It was as if powers were at war beyond the reach of my senses, beyond nature . . . unreal phantoms, coils of fog, primeval shadows . . .

Nina stood breathless at my side, her hands pressed to her mouth. In the night-darkness I could see that her eyes were closed; for her, too, the battle was one of shadows, the real battle somewhere else.

The end was inevitable; the desperate, whipping movements of the snake began to subside, to grow slower and slower; little by little the coiling, twisting body ceased to struggle, shuddered convulsively, and relaxed, the great cougar crouched among the coils, pinning them to earth . . .

I heard Nina give a sob beside me; but when I turned to her, she was gone. I could hear her running through the night, through the trees, in the direction of the house. "Nina!" I called; but she didn't answer.

I shone the light on the battlefield once more, but there was nothing there; the space was empty. With a beating heart I went closer, to look: the bushes were trampled, flattened; a low branch was broken from a tree.

On the ground, in the torch-light, as though thrown there, lay an old piece of frayed rope.

CHAPTER

15

I followed Nina back to Stonecliff, the torch lighting my way among the trees. I half expected the house to be dark, but long before I got there, I could see the glow of its lights through the fog. It loomed up, misty and insubstantial, like a sorcerer's tower; as though something strange and fearful were about to issue from it.

I was determined to have it out with Granville then and there. Nina was mine by all the laws of nature, his hold on her perverse and unnatural. His need for her had held her in some kind of spell, and now it was time to put an end to it. Love was stronger than an old man's need; that had been proven to me that night.

But when, in this desperate mood, I burst into the house, I found it no different from before. All was as usual, warm and peaceful; a fire was burning in the fireplace, the lamps were lit, and Granville was at his desk, bent over his manuscript, a full glass and a half-empty bottle in front of him.

I wanted no more evasion and mystery. "Where is Nina?" I demanded.

He looked up from his writing, obviously weary. He was unshaven, and his hand, as he reached for the glass, trembled a little. "She is not here," he said.

In no mood to be humble or polite, I planted myself in front of him. "What have you done with her?" I asked.

He looked up at me, his head hunched between his shoulders; and I thought of a snake, coiled to strike . . . "You will not find her," he said. "She is in transition."

"Then wherever that is," I ordered, "bring her back."

He raised the glass to his lips and took a long swallow. "To the young," he said, "everything is so simple. They ask, 'where are you?' . . . and the answer is 'here! . . . I am over here!' 'Then here I come,' they cry, 'ready or not!' "

"I demand to see her."

"Oh," he said, "you will see her. As a matter of fact, she wants to see you. But not until tomorrow. As she really is."

"I know what she really is," I said. "I know that I love her, and that she loves me."

He smiled a little sadly. "It must seem so to you," he said. "And perhaps, after all, you are right . . . she loves you. For a moment."

"Let her tell me herself that it's for a moment!"

He sighed. "She is not what you imagine, Mr. Robb," he said. "She is not a young girl. She is a woman."

"I know that already," I told him.

I saw with satisfaction that I had made him wince. "That was unnecessary," he said, not without a certain dignity; and for a moment I felt almost sorry for him.

But I had no intention of being trapped by pity. I remembered that in the hands of a wizard, the blade is always somewhere else. "She belongs to me now," I said. "Because of tonight."

He nodded somberly. "Yes," he said, "I was afraid you must think so."

He brooded quietly, his fingers playing on the bottle. "But unfortunately, I need her, Mr. Robb," he said at last. "As she really is.

"You do not understand that, I suppose."

"I don't understand anything at all," I told him. "Except that Nina is flesh and blood, and not a piece of old rope."

"Rope?" he murmured, obviously puzzled; "rope? . . . Oh!" His face cleared. "Yes—of course. You have seen Max."

"What there was left of him," I said shortly. "Some chewed-up hemp."

Nodding, he glanced for a moment at the sheet of paper in front of him. "Yes," he said slowly, more to himself than to me; "that was the way it had to come out."

He looked up and smiled. "We must find something else for him," he said.

There was a long pause while he stared at the night outside his windows. "I am a selfish old man," he said after a while. "But then—I have to be."

Turning, he faced me, his head cocked to one side. "Are you selfish, too, Mr. Robb?" he asked; and answered himself: "Yes—I suppose you are."

He raised an admonitory finger, like a schoolmaster. "It is necessary for a wizard to be selfish, Mr. Robb," he said. "Or for a writer; I make no distinction between them. To move people . . ."

I could feel myself slipping back under the spell of Granville's world again . . . once more half-believing the unbelievable. I made a last effort to stay angry, and out of it. "Do what you please with your own people," I said; "but I'm not one of them."

"I know," said Granville sadly. "I should never have let you come here in the first place."

"Nina isn't one of your people either," I told him.

He studied me with what, to my surprise, seemed like compassion. "Sit down, Michael," he said at last: "It can do you no good to quarrel with me."

I sat down, but unwillingly. "You said I'd see her tomorrow," I reminded him. "Will you let her go then?"

He looked uncomfortable for a moment. "If you both feel then as you did tonight . . ." he began, and left the sentence hanging in mid-air.

"I want to marry her," I said.

I felt ridiculous, like a young suitor asking a girl's father for her hand. It helped to make me angry again.

"Well," I demanded; "haven't you anything to say?"

He shrugged his shoulders. "It is all sea-foam," he said.

"It's real," I told him. "You'd better understand that."

"Very well," he said calmly; "You can propose to her tomorrow."

"Why not tonight? Are you afraid?"

"Yes," he said. And he added wryly,

"Work with the heart is very delicate, Mr. Robb. One cannot always be sure. Merlin himself was boxed in a tree."

In my excited state I half expected him to disappear in a puff of smoke at that moment. But he only rose wearily from his desk, and taking his bottle and his glass with him, started slowly out of the room and up the stairs. "Goodnight, Mr. Robb," he said.

"She wants to leave you," I called out after him. "I heard her crying, 'Let me go!'"

"You didn't understand that, either," he said.

CHAPTER

16

My last night at Stonecliff was like my first. The sound of silence hummed in my ears, and an owl hooted somewhere among the crags. I paced up and down in my room for what seemed hours; I was tense and uneasy, one moment angry, and then just as suddenly stabbed by anxiety. A thousand plans, hopes, fears whirled through my mind; I couldn't wait for morning to come, yet for some reason—was it a presentiment?—I didn't want to let go of the night; I wanted to hold it back, not to let it pass.

And the morning, too, was like the first morning: there was a fog along the coast, and the ashes of last night's fire were gray in the fireplace. There was no sign of the Mexican woman; the kitchen looked dim and forbidding. I got myself a glass of water, and went out onto the terrace and sat down to wait.

The terrace was wet, bare, and fog-shrouded. I hugged my jacket around me, feeling the cold in my bones. A foghorn bellowed faintly somewhere along the coast.

And then Nina came out of the house, and started across the terrace toward me.

Nina? Was it Nina—? that silver-haired woman?

She stopped a little way off from me, and we stared at each other—I, in utter consternation, she, gently studying me, her eyes beseeching and a little sad. "Yes," she said after awhile; "I am Nina. And I am Virginia Granville."

I couldn't speak. All my hopes, plans, dreams, shattered in my skull like so many bits of glass. Bewilderment robbed me of all movement; I could only stand and stare. Even my blood seemed to have stopped moving.

"Come," she said; "let me make you some breakfast." It was Nina's voice, but the young-girl sound had gone out of it.

Numbly, unable to say a word, I followed her across the terrace and into the kitchen.

Thrown loosely over her shoulders was the same sweater she had been wearing the first time I saw her. And in the kitchen there was the same odor of coffee and bacon in the air, and the other odor, too—that faint fragrance like delicate tea. Only, now her honey-dark hair was almost white, and caught up in a twist at the nape of her neck. There were tiny lines at the corners of her eyes, and near her mouth—that warm, seeking mouth!

—the full cheeks sagged just a little. She was Nina, and she was Virginia Granville; and she was sixty years old.

I found my voice finally, from somewhere—where, I didn't know. "So it was a spell after all," I said. I must have sounded like an angry child, because she placed her hand over mine for a moment, in a comforting gesture. It was a well-worn hand, a little dry, and the knuckles were swollen.

"You must forgive him, Michael," she said. "He has been unhappy, too."

Unhappy? I thought dully. What had he to be unhappy about?

"But why, Nina?" I asked. "Why?"

"Virginia," she reminded me.

"Virginia, then—"

What had happened to her? What had happened to us both? Was my whole stay at Stonecliff nothing but a dream?

She smiled suddenly, and it was Nina's smile, clear and sweet. "I'm sorry, Michael," she said. "He wanted things to come out differently; he wanted to write it so beautifully, for Max."

"Max," I said: "that old man in the tree-house. Was he to have the girl?"

"Yes," she said. "But then you came along. And he saw that he couldn't write it that way any more."

"When did he realize that? Last night?"

"Yes," she said steadily.

"I see." But of course, I didn't, I didn't see at

all. "Tell me," I said: "what spell did he put on you? On us?"

She smiled gently. "Do you think a writer can't turn his wife into a young girl?" she asked.

"So it was all sea-foam after all," I said. "He made it up—out of fog and rain and flowering bushes . . ."

"And out of love," she said.

"Did he love this girl Halys?"

"There is no Halys," she said. "He loves the young girl in her."

"Then why did he need Nina?"

She looked at me quietly. "Without her," she said, "he would have forgotten what he was in love with."

I felt empty and tired. "Whatever he did," I said bitterly, "he did it too well."

"He did indeed," she agreed. "He almost lost me."

A very small spark leaped for a moment somewhere in my blood. "Then I wasn't wrong about last night," I exclaimed. It seemed terribly important to know that there had been some reality in what I had felt, in what had happened . . . that there was some truth, somewhere . . .

She looked away, and I could see a blush starting at her neck and moving upward to her cheeks. "Let's say that I found myself with feelings that I didn't know I had," she said quietly.

"But you begged him to let you go!" I cried, clutching at some last, vain hope; "you asked him to release you!"

"Yes," she said, "to release me. But not from him. From the girl Nina . . . to let me go back to being me again, before it was too late."

I stared at her, still only half convinced. She made a little helpless gesture with her hands. "He said you wouldn't understand," she said.

"No," I admitted; "I don't. I wish I did."

She looked at me for what seemed a long time. In her face I saw many things: wisdom, and kindness—but most of all peace.

"You will some day," she said gently. "When you have written your own love stories."

She seemed beautiful to me, as beautiful as when I had first seen her as a young girl coming across the patio toward me. That was how she must have looked long ago, I thought; I hadn't fallen in love with an illusion, it was only a skipped beat in time. That was what she had been like when Edward fell in love with her, thirty years before; and if I had been in Provincetown then, or in Paris, I'd have fallen in love with her, too. And she might have loved me and chosen me instead of Edward. It would have been Michael and Virginia then—or Michael and Nina—with all their lives ahead of them: the beginning writer, and the young actress. And our first avowals would have been no different from last night's breathless seeking . . . Thirty years ago.

I wanted to think so, and I thought so, and it was a comfort to me. Already I had forgiven Granville; he had only done what he had been obliged to do. Perhaps he had moved me, also—

but I forgave him for that, too. Perhaps, as Virginia said, some day I would move my own people.

Still—he could scarcely have turned her into Nina without her help. "You must have been willing," I said.

"Of course," she admitted. "After all, I love him. It was the least I could do."

She was serene, fulfilled, content with life and with her place in it. "This is the best time," she said; "When I'm myself."

"For a while," I said, "I thought you were Nimue. He thought so too, I think . . . once or twice . . ."

She looked placidly out across the terrace to the sea, still lost in fog. "That is a wife's only advantage," she said.

"Then you did help him, Nina-Virginia?"

She seemed to be smiling gently to herself. "A wife also does things with the heart," she said.

It is six months, now, since I left Stonecliff. I am sitting at my desk with the last page of the biography in front of me. What am I to call it? I do not know. "A Wizard Does Things With The Heart"?

Or, more simply—"Nina"?

I shall never forget her. Yet—what is there to remember? Something—someone—that never was. A masque of young women. A dreaming of nymphs.

Who was the wizard—Granville, or Virginia?

Was it his love for her, or hers for him, that laid a spell on Stonecliff and on me? Did I imagine it all? Was it nothing but illusion? Yet, if so—how could I have been on the fire-beach that night with that boy and that girl?

On my desk, among my papers, there is a review of Granville's latest novel, clipped from the Sunday *Times*. According to the reviewer, it is a story about an elderly painter named Max, and a young man, his pupil, named Jon. The reviewer quotes in part from the book:

"There, at night, the fires burn yellow and bright in the blue, sea-evening air; families bend over their cooking, children play, and couples wander in and out of shadow and firelight, up and down across the sand, or lie together near the flames, screened by a blanket against the night wind from the sea."

The reviewer then continues:

"As Max and Jon sit by their fire-ring one evening, there stumbles into their firelight a girl . . . named Halys . . ."